Keishi Ayasato

Illustration by
Saki Ukai

Torture Princess

Fremd Torturchen

"I am the **Torture Princess,** Elisabeth Le Fanu.

I am the proud wolf and the lowly sow."

"O Sinless Soul, stricken down in a manner most foul. From this day forth, you shall be my loyal servant."

Although it made little sense to demand the servitude of a dead man, her tone left no room for refusal. Belatedly, Kaito realized that he was breathing, and as he let slip a small chuckle of confusion, the girl before him made a dignified proclamation.

Kaito Sena

"I approve!"

Elisabeth smiled, her expression gleaming with satisfaction, as if to tell him that he was capable of anything he set his mind to. For a moment, Kaito envisioned a pair of cat ears flopping atop her luxurious black hair.

Elisabeth

"Welcome home, Master Kaito! I have awaited your safe return!"

Hina ✦

Contained within these pages is the record of a loathsome sinner.
It is the account of a woman who will die alone, forsaken by all of creation.

O Lord, forgive us our sins.
O Lord, have mercy, for we are imperfect.
When we can no longer shoulder the burden of our own filth, burn it away with flame and suffering.

The vile woman. The famished wolf. The greedy sow.
May the flames deliver her from sin.

When the time comes, may You grant her punishment so that she may atone for her sins with tears of blood.
For Your mercy is boundless, and You hear even the prayers of sinners.

Please lend her Your ear until her screams of atonement fade into nothingness.
For forgiveness exists with You, and so it is You who we worship and fear.

O Lord, please save her soul from the ashes.

O sinful Torture Princess—Elisabeth Le Fanu.
Until the day comes—until the day of your death—try to do some good at least.

Excerpt from the introduction to *Records of the Torture Princess*

1

Keishi Ayasato

illustration by
Saki Ukai

Torture Princess

Fremd Torturchen

YEN ON

New York

Keishi Ayasato

Illustration by
Saki Ukai

Translation by Nathaniel Hiroshi Thrasher
Cover art by Saki Ukai

ISEKAI GOMON HIME Volume 1 Fremd Torturchen
©Keishi Ayasato 2016
First published in Japan in 2016 by KADOKAWA CORPORATION, Tokyo.
English translation rights arranged with KADOKAWA CORPORATION, Tokyo,
through TUTTLE-MORI AGENCY, INC., Tokyo.

English translation © 2019 by Yen Press, LLC

Yen On
1290 Avenue of the Americas
New York, NY 10104

Visit us at yenpress.com
facebook.com/yenpress
twitter.com/yenpress
yenpress.tumblr.com
instagram.com/yenpress

First Yen On Edition: May 2019

Yen On is an imprint of Yen Press, LLC.
The Yen On name and logo are trademarks of Yen Press, LLC.

The publisher is not responsible for websites (or their content) that are not owned by the publisher.

Library of Congress Cataloging-in-Publication Data
Names: Ayasato, Keishi, author. | Ukai, Saki, illustrator. | Thrasher, Nathaniel Hiroshi, translator.
Title: Torture princess: fremd torturchen / Keishi Ayasato ; illustration by Saki Ukai ;
    translation by Nathaniel Hiroshi Thrasher.
Other titles: Isekai gomon hime. English
Description: First Yen On edition. | New York, NY : Yen On, 2019–
Identifiers: LCCN 2019005330 | ISBN 9781975304690 (v. 1 : pbk.)
Classification: LCC PL867.5.Y36 I8413 2019 | DDC 895.63/6—dc23
LC record available at https://lccn.loc.gov/2019005330

ISBNs: 978-1-9753-0469-0 (paperback)
        978-1-9753-0470-6 (ebook)

10 9 8 7 6 5 4 3 2 1

LSC-C

Printed in the United States of America

Contents

Prologue

As the hands around his neck tightened, Kaito Sena mused on how predictable this outcome was.

In fact, it was a miracle that he had lived this long in the first place. His right arm was covered in shallow lacerations, his left arm unmoving and stained dark red. His ankle had been twisted at an odd angle a few months back and had stiffened that way. And it was possible that the stomach pain he had been enduring for the past three days was due to one of his organs having ruptured.

He was seventeen years and three months old. All through his life, he'd only known fickle treatment and been attacked on a whim.

It was a life no better than that of livestock, knowing it would eventually be devoured yet unable to escape its fate. In his case, he wasn't going to be eaten but rather buried alive somewhere, or perhaps his flesh would be burned away until only bone remained, or maybe his body would be abandoned in the mountains or dumped in the ocean.

The pain weighed heavily on him as time seemed to stretch longer and longer. While he was thinking, the fat fingers pressed down on his neck even harder, crushing his respiratory tract and blood vessels. Sticky tears leaked from his protruding eyeballs.

He kicked and clawed at the hands grabbing him, but it was no use. His father was doped up well past the point of being able to reason or feel pain. As Kaito's tongue lolled out in his desperate attempt to struggle for one more lungful of air, a part of him separated from his body and observed the situation with a disturbing level of calm. His brain, on the other hand, was burning with panic. *I don't want to die I don't want to die I don't want to die I don't want to die please don't kill me.*

Against his wishes, his throat gave in. His vision went blank, but rather than infinite blackness, he saw a dancing light.

It was almost like his life was flashing before his eyes, like in stories.

But this was something else entirely, something sinister.

There were corpses as far as the eye could see.

There were men and women, young and old, their bodies mutilated and cast aside. Their hands and feet had been twisted off like those of broken dolls, their chests ripped open, their limbs torn off. Eyes, ears, teeth, and tongues were all missing.

Before Kaito's eyes lay a mountain of corpses, each lacking so much as a shred of human dignity.

A crow cawed before taking flight, a lump of human flesh in its beak. Kaito's vision darkened, and he could hear the roar of countless voices. A mass of people, clad in black and shaking their fists, shouted as high as their voices would allow. "Kill her! Kill her! Kill her! Kill her! Kill her! Kill her!"

All their loathing and overwhelming bloodlust were concentrated on one dark-haired girl.

She was hovering in front of them, dressed in a straitjacket.

Hundreds of chains hung from the gallows, binding her hands and feet while keeping her suspended in midair. She resembled a butterfly caught in a spiderweb. She looked up from her fluttering black locks.

Her face was terrifying in its beauty, and her striking crimson eyes turned to Kaito. He gasped.

It was clear from her expression that she was no victim.

She was looking past Kaito at the raging, bloodthirsty crowd. Her pointed gaze was devoid of fear.

Upon her immaculate face was a smile rife with cruelty and wickedness.

"Kill her! Kill her! Kill her!" The mob continued their chant, and she laughed as she bathed in their murderous rage. She laughed at it all in a manner both beautiful and sinister.

—*Until the day of your death, try to do some good at least.*

And then, with a firm *crack*, Kaito Sena's neck was snapped.

Kaito Sena, the boy who should be dead, opened his eyes once more. The light of a bonfire filled his gaze. He appeared to be in a dimly lit stone room. Although he was sure that he'd been killed, this didn't quite strike him as the land of the dead. Standing in front of the confused Kaito was the black-haired girl from before.

She was no longer being restrained, although in a sense, she still appeared bound.

Covering her slender body was a black bondage dress, and the part over her chest was composed almost entirely of leather belts.

Her well-formed breasts, bound beneath the interlacing belts, were over half-visible. Her waist was concealed by black cloth, and past her short skirt extended a pair of gorgeous legs wrapped in what looked like stockings. The inside of her dress was dyed scarlet, and the length of the back flowed like a cape. It was quite the erotic outfit, yet somehow it did not give off a flirty impression.

The way she wore the indecent bondage-style dress was akin to a queen in her finest regalia.

Her elegant, flowing black hair suited her face, which was more refined than any Kaito had seen before. Yet, a demonic cruelty flickered in her ruby eyes.

At once, the peerless beauty parted her thin lips. Her gaze locked on to Kaito, and she spoke at last.

"O Sinless Soul, stricken down in a manner most foul. From this day forth, you shall be my loyal servant."

Although it made little sense to demand the servitude of a dead man, her tone left no room for refusal. Belatedly, Kaito realized that he was breathing, and as he let slip a small chuckle of confusion, the girl before him made a dignified proclamation.

"I am the Torture Princess, Elisabeth Le Fanu. I am the proud wolf and the lowly sow."

1
The
Fourteen
Demons

Fremd Torkürchen

The castle stood atop a desolate hill, surrounded on all sides by dense forest. It was constructed wholly from frigid stone and, as such, resembled a fortress more than it did a castle.

It gave off an oppressive air, and most anyone who spent more than three days inside it would be plagued by nightmares of being crushed by stones. Its corridors were labyrinthine, and if one got lost in them, there was a greater chance of starving to death before finding a way out. It wasn't built with the comfort of its inhabitants in mind; in fact, it seemed to reject the idea of being inhabited altogether.

Its kitchen was no different. The layout was abysmal, and its atmosphere evoked the claustrophobic sense of being locked in a dungeon.

Not to mention the nature of the ingredients that had been forced upon him.

Kaito Sena wore a cotton shirt with rolled-up sleeves and a butcher's apron. His arms were crossed and he bore a sullen expression. Before him lay a towering mound of organs. The varied bits of flesh were all soft and glistening and gave off a strong, peculiar odor.

He sighed and, with a sharp knife, began cutting the intestines lengthwise. He then removed the white bits from the heart. As he was dressing the vast quantity of meat with sage-like stoicism, the kitchen shook violently. Kaito ignored this, acting as though nothing had happened.

Even if the castle was to collapse and his life was to end, it was of little concern to him.

He took the expensive-looking bottle he'd randomly grabbed from the wine cellar, opened it, and poured its contents into a silver fruit bowl. At once, he began dumping the organ meat into the bowl along with some herbs he couldn't identify.

His face stern, he continued cooking even as the entire castle shook again. Once more, he ignored it. Even if half the castle was blown away, Kaito would still be fine, so he paid no attention to the tremors. His world was at peace. However, a wicked voice rang out and shattered that tranquility.

"Butler! Buuutler!"

His name was in fact Kaito and not Butler. Thus, he decided the voice couldn't possibly be calling for him. Under that justification, he continued ignoring it, but then the manner in which he was being called changed.

"Kaaaiiito!"

"All right, all right! I'm coming right now, so pipe down!"

His life was at risk if he continued playing deaf. He slammed the liver he was flouring onto the counter, then took off down the corridor. Thanks to the poor excuses for stained-glass clerestory windows, the corridor was less claustrophobic than the kitchen. At the same time, the patterns of light they cast on the floor were ominous enough to be annoying. He ran atop the patterns, climbed a spiral staircase, and finally threw open a massive pair of double doors.

A violent gust of wind blew in Kaito's face. The throne room, as the name would suggest, was adorned with a magnificent throne atop a pedestal, and the array of antique tapestries served to accentuate the room's grandeur. However, a quarter of the room had been destroyed, and the pale-blue sky peeked through a huge hole in the wall.

It seemed there was a serious chance that half the castle had been blown away.

Standing above the wreckage, an arrogant girl awaited Kaito, her arms folded and her perfectly sculpted legs perched atop the rubble. Her heels clicked as she turned to face him.

Her dark hair fluttered around her as she pierced him with her crimson gaze.

Her face, a well of inhuman beauty, was punctuated by a smile dripping with unfettered delight. It was truly unpleasant. Her nails were painted black, and they glimmered as she pointed outside. She spoke in a whisper, her voice as sweet as birdsong with the tone of a cat that had just eaten its fill.

"Behold, Kaito."

Kaito obeyed and peered through the hole. The bright-blue sky and vivid-green forest would have been picturesque were it not for the sticky red that stained the landscape, accompanied by the stench of rust. The once-beautiful setting was now a sickening sight to behold.

A nightmarish hellscape stretched as far as the eye could see.

Dozens of iron stakes jutted out of the ground, impaling a strange creature.

Kaito scrunched up his face as much as he could, but he could still make out the grizzly, bloodied corpses.

"Well, Kaito? Have you any impressions?"

"Impressions...? It's revolting."

"A fitting appraisal, truly. What's more, it lacks the requisite vocabulary and wit to entertain its master. What a boring creature."

The girl shrugged. The dying beast was a horrifying patchwork of human corpses. It was a bizarre creature, its skin a collage of human faces with their cheeks and scalps melted together and stretched to the absolute limit. Each face joined its voice in a chorus of agony. A row of human arms along its back served as a mane, and a large number of breasts hung from its fat belly.

The girl laughed at the blasphemous abomination, her voice full of scorn.

"The time has come, Kaito. The Knight has issued a declaration of war. Or would it be more fitting to consider this mere harassment?"

She seemed quite pleased. Watching her lick her garnet lips, Kaito thought she looked less like a panther or a wolf and more like a ferocious, hungry lion. Suppressing his urge to vomit, he looked away from the beast's corpse and gave his announcement through a sigh.

"Not that I really care, but food'll be ready in an hour. Save your fighting or torturing or whatever for later."

This was the absurd arrangement Kaito Sena had been forced into after he was killed.

✳

"As you have yet to reply, I shall say it another way. Devote yourself to me."

"Hard pass."

★　　★　　★

When he registered the blunt demand of the girl who called herself Elisabeth, Kaito immediately refused. Naturally, he was confused at being ordered to do some strange girl's bidding immediately after he'd been killed. But he was sure of his answer after seeing that disturbing pile of corpses. Then there were the bloodthirsty chants that had been directed at her, plus Elisabeth's sadistic smile, but most of all, it was that she addressed herself as the "Torture Princess."

He was afraid he'd made her angry, but for some reason, she nodded as if impressed.

"A prompt decision, I see. Did you perchance stumble across a stray memory or two of mine when you were summoned? Even so, I did not expect such a swift reply."

"Okay, forget the whole 'serving you' thing for a sec. When you say 'summoned'... Hey wait, where are we? What am I doing here? Didn't I...die?"

"Yes, without a doubt! You are well and truly dead. Your murder was as meaningless as a worm getting stepped on—a death most pitiful, unseemly, cruel, and gruesome! Yet, I summoned your soul here into a puppet body and granted you new life. A rare blessing, is it not? Go on, then: Rejoice to your heart's content."

"...A puppet?"

As he listened to Elisabeth's bizarre explanation, Kaito patted himself all over. For a puppet, his skin felt surprisingly human. He didn't have a mirror, so he couldn't inspect his face, but noting the lack of discrepancies in his field of view, he suspected that his height was more or less the same as it had always been. He plucked out one of his hairs, which he normally kept tied behind his head, but it was the same old pale brown.

As Kaito inspected his body with a dubious expression, Elisabeth spoke again, exasperated.

"Now listen here, you. The body housing your soul is a golem of my own creation. It isn't one of those lumps of dirt that will die simply from having part of the word on its forehead erased. It is a superlative piece of work, for I am both a master sorcerer and a skilled artisan. It's thanks to my handiwork that you're hearing me in the language of your land, too. And the frame is unquestionably robust. It has organs and blood, true, but so long as it remains at least fifty percent intact, you can consider it immortal. Ah well, the blood coursing through your veins has been mixed with my own, so I suppose that if the body bleeds out, your soul will dissipate."

"But my build, my hair color, all of it's the same."

"It seems your idiocy is beyond help. I already spoke of my skill, did I not? Do not lump my masterpiece in with bargain-shop refuse. If you put a soul in a container that differs too greatly from the form of its previous life, the dissonance can cause madness. The body is designed to transform according to the inhabiting soul. It automatically eliminates wounds and disease, but the appearance and build are the same as yours, from the face that reflects your impoverished nature to your gaunt, brittle frame. Feel free to weep at my compassion."

It was then that Kaito noticed the major change in his body. Looking at his arm, he realized that the scarring and lacerations that had once been etched into it were now gone without a trace. The pain, previously his lifelong companion, had completely vanished.

Huh… That's a surprise. This really isn't my body after all.

Kaito finally accepted it. There was no way this agony-free

body could be his. Not being in pain for the first time in a while was certainly pleasant, but at the same time, it made him feel uneasy, like he was a plastic doll or something.

As Kaito cradled his arm in amazement, Elisabeth carried on.

"I summoned a Sinless Soul to use as a servant. The Church would punish me if they found out I invoked anything evil, even if only to use it as a maid, you see. You fit the criteria, as your death was far crueler than your sins in life would warrant, but... Heh, there *was* some odd resistance during the summoning, but to think that you would hail from another world... I wonder whether pulling you in from a parallel dimension is the height of fortune or misfortune? Ah, I suppose it matters little who you once were. From here on, you need only serve me with whole-hearted devotion."

"Hard pass."

"Oh-ho."

Elisabeth narrowed her crimson eyes, apparently pleased by his response. Her long, slender finger resembled a blade as she raised Kaito's chin. Licking her lips, she whispered in a voice that was sweet nectar.

"You were killed. Your murder was as meaningless as a worm getting stepped on—a death most pitiful, unseemly, cruel, and gruesome. Even your hollow little brain understands that much, yes? Your death was far crueler than your sins in life would warrant, fulfilling the requirement to become a Sinless Soul, yet you wear the face of a man about to descend into Hell. Even so, you would give up this second life? You would choose to die, crushed like a worm?"

"Oh yeah, for sure. I've had enough abuse for one lifetime. I endured and persisted, sure, but surviving isn't really the same as *living*. I'm done."

Kaito gave his response. Without even needing to think about it, he could say that it had been a terrible life.

He'd attended school for a couple of years. Afterward, he'd been forced to move from place to place and help his father with his illegal work. When that had taken a turn south and his manpower was no longer needed, his father began beating him to let off steam. All in all, it was a sickening way to live. Kaito didn't even remember what his mother looked like. But he suspected that her brain had been addled by pain and malnutrition, robbing her of the willpower to flee, and eventually she'd been killed much like himself.

He was thankful for his new pain-free body, but he'd be damned if he let himself be used by anyone else again. If his shitty life was prolonged, all that meant was that he would have to endure even more shit.

"I've had enough. I'm throwing in the towel. Go find someone else to be your servant."

"I see. Well, like it or not, I'll make a butler out of you yet."

Once again, Kaito's reply was completely ignored. His frown deepened as Elisabeth shrugged.

"Summoning more servants would result in the Church casting their bothersome gaze my way. And crafting another puppet would take time. What sense is there in creating more chores for the sake of a servant, whose role it is to do my chores for me? I cannot think of a greater waste of time. At any rate, of—"

Suddenly, there was a roar as the door behind Elisabeth burst off its hinges.

The way in which the thick, heavy door spun through the air before finally crashing beside her was almost comical. A splinter grazed her cheek, yet she didn't even turn to look. Kaito's eyes widened in fear as he gawked at the entrance.

There in the doorway—minus one door—stood a colossal horse and its rider.

For reins, the rider held a sinister thorned chain, and the saddle it was mounted on was made of bone. But strangest of all were the bodies. Neither the horse nor the rider had any skin. They looked like anatomical models, their muscles bare and their bodies lined with blood vessels. With their flesh pink and glistening, they were hideous enough that the mind refused to parse them out of self-preservation.

Finally turning toward the entrance, Elisabeth began speaking with an air of leisure.

"At any rate, of the fourteen ranked demons—the Knight, the Governor, the Grand Governor, the Earl, the Grand Earl, the Duke, the Grand Duke, the Marquis, the Grand Marquis, the Monarch, the Grand Monarch, the King, the Grand King, and the Kaiser—leaving out the Kaiser, who's already been captured, I have thirteen demons and their contractors I need to slaughter."

The horse let out a whinny, and the rider roared again. Their mouths were simply hollow gaps in their flesh, and from them came the grating noise of a storm passing through a broken wind instrument. As the shriek of hatred rang in his eardrums, Kaito suddenly understood something and was certain of it.

Demon was the only fitting word to describe this horrifying creature.

"Hey, what's up with that guy? Is he the 'Knight' you just mentioned?"

"For an imbecile who died a worm's death, you seem surprisingly calm."

"As long as my brain isn't atrophied, I can at least make sound decisions."

"Well, you were close. That there is a servant of the Knight. He didn't form a contract with a demon himself but became the underling of one who did. By choice. A weakling, in other words. Both he and the Knight used to be human, though."

Listening to Elisabeth's explanation, Kaito felt his gaze wander over to the horse and rider again. He couldn't believe that the rider used to be human, nor did he want to. Only a lunatic would willingly become something like that. Guessing Kaito's thought process from the look on his face, Elisabeth snickered.

"Your reaction is understandable. Quite unsavory, no? Selling one's soul to a demon and abandoning one's form, all in the pursuit of inhuman power, is rather pitiful, is it not? You may laugh. I shall allow it. 'Tis his wish, no doubt—after all, buffoonery is buffoonery precisely because it inspires laughter, wouldn't you agree?"

Even as provocation, her words were raw. The rider let out another, more piercing roar. The rage in his voice was so high-pitched that Kaito had to cover his ears for fear of his eardrums rupturing.

The rider yanked the reins and kicked the horse's flank. The horse accelerated to its top speed in an instant, cracking the stone floor as it charged toward Elisabeth in an attempt to trample her.

"Lowborn dirt. My blade is too good for the likes of you—*Iron Maiden*."

Elisabeth mouthed something and extended her hand. Darkness and bloodred flower petals flowed from her fingertips and swirled through the air. There was a loud *gong* and then a life-size puppet sprang up from the ground and cut through the darkness.

The puppet, which Elisabeth had called Iron Maiden, looked far kinder than the name would suggest.

Golden thread that served as hair hung down its back, and the jewels that adorned its face in place of eyes glittered blue. Its lips curled into a warm, loving smile. As it opened its arms in welcome, the rider bore down upon it, consumed by fury.

It was right when Kaito thought the horse would trample over the Maiden's kind embrace that it happened.

In concert with the clicking sound of shifting gears, the puppet opened its eyes wide. The blue jewels flipped over, now burning scarlet. Its affection forgotten, its expression turned to hatred, and its stomach opened with a *click*.

A pair of iron arms shot out from the inside, each equipped with long, vicious claws. Scrabbling forth, they swooped down on the horse and its rider, smashing arms and legs with a cold malevolence and mechanical efficiency. The desperate cries of the horse and rider fell on deaf ears as the arms mashed their victims' extremities into caterpillar-like lumps of flesh.

The horse and rider were unable to put up any sort of resistance, and after being sculpted into a grotesque form resembling a meatball with a head, they were carried into the Maiden's stomach. As if to symbolize its chastity, its womb was lined with countless needles.

"GYYAAAAAAAAAAAAAAAAAAAAAAAAAAHHHHHHH!"
Ignoring the screams of pain, the Maiden's chest clicked closed.

As its expression became affectionate once more, the Maiden lovingly embraced her belly. The crazed screams coming from inside it begged for release. Just listening to them made Kaito feel like he was going mad, too.

"Once one enters Iron Maiden, death does not come quickly."

Elisabeth spoke over the horrifying screams, clearly unbothered. Turning toward Kaito, she offered a suggestive smile.

"If you insist on dying again, then there's no helping it. I am nothing if not generous, after all, so I will grant your wish. But I will not simply return you to a state of death. If you desire death so badly, you will have it by way of *my* methods. So. What path will you choose? Will you become my butler, or will you become meat?"

"Butler, please."

"Well, that was fast."

That was how Kaito came to serve the Torture Princess. Which brings us to the present.

"This! Is! Vile!"

In tandem with this spirited protest, the heart roast with potherb garnish and fruit vinegar sauce Kaito had made went flying through the air, accompanied by plate and fork. A dangerous rain of food and cutlery pelted the antique tablecloth.

Continuing her tirade, Elisabeth planted a foot on the table with a *stomp*.

"Wh-what *is* this? It's absolutely repulsive. It looks palatable, yet the meat is undercooked, and it has the texture of rubber. The sauce somehow takes on the organ's peculiar odor, and the odd sweet and sour flavors create a horrific harmony that lingers on the tongue. It's almost impressive, in a way."

"Your description is what's impressive."

With dead eyes, Kaito yanked the fork out of the wall it had impaled. He wondered where she found the nerve to give such harsh criticism.

A few days had passed since he'd been strong-armed into becoming her butler. Such outbursts had scared him at first, but given that he'd lived his whole life a hairbreadth from death anyway, he quickly got used to it.

Still clad in his unflattering butler uniform, Kaito heaved a sigh.

"Like I keep saying, you don't need to throw it at me. What are you, some abusive husband from the sixties?"

"I know not of any sixty abusive husbands, but food that vile deserves to be thrown! What do you call this?! It is so unpalatable even pig fodder would be preferable! How is it that all your dishes are this vile?!"

"You kept complaining about the odor, so I thought I'd try using wine this time to offset it."

"...Hold on. Do you mean to tell me that you used my prized wine to create this *filth*?"

Kaito decided that silence was golden. Not needing an answer, Elisabeth waved her hand.

A chair sprang up beneath Kaito's feet with a *gong*. He looked almost like a character in a cartoon as it scooped up his rear, then fastened him in place with belts. When he looked, it was clear that the seat and armrests were lined with holes made for needles, pins, and spikes. Abandoning his cool demeanor, he kicked his legs in a panic.

"Wait, wait, wait, wait, wait! Let's talk this over. Think about it. I've never cooked *anything* before, and you're asking me to cook *organs?*"

"Save your excuses. As an aside, is that any way to talk to me, the Torture Princess? You have some nerve. Perhaps you'll have time to reflect on your arrogance as you're being riddled with holes, hmm?"

"I'm sorry! Look, ever since I got killed, it's been kind of hard to register feelings like fear or danger! I'm sorry, okay? Can we just skip the torture?"

"Very well. I shall grant you mercy...or so I would like to say, but do you mean to tell me that you only respect me out of fear?"

"Well, uh, that's not...*not* true..."

"What, no excuse, then, Kaaaito?"

As he shouted that he wanted to take it back, Kaito's fate dawned on him. He was going to become a human pincushion. However, Elisabeth seemed to reconsider, and as she snorted, the Iron Chair vanished.

"Very well. In my infinite generosity, I shall grant you one last chance—I demand pudding."

"...Pudding?"

Her comical order was placed with a straight face, and Kaito cocked his head in puzzlement. Elisabeth nodded, then crossed her legs and leaned back in her chair, her face full of conviction.

"I have my doubts as to whether a fool who can't even cook will be able to handle confectionery, you see. But perhaps you'll have a knack for sweets. It won't hurt to try. And if even that is beyond you, then, like anything that does naught but produce trash, you will simply be disposed of."

"Please don't talk about disposing of people. It hits a little too close to home. Pudding, right? I think I know what you're talking about... Though where I'm from, it sounds more like *purin*."

"*Purin*? I know not of this dish, but from the sound of the name, there should at least be a vague similarity, no?"

Kaito nodded at her half-hearted answer. As a matter of fact, he had strong memories associated with that dish.

Long ago, the woman living with his father at the time had served it for young Kaito. He'd been overjoyed, and she met his glee with a forced smile. The next day, she was gone. Thinking back on it, he realized that it had probably been meant as atonement for leaving him behind and escaping on her own. Even now, the memory of that rare moment of happiness was vivid. And he more or less remembered how she'd made it.

He could re-create it with the ingredients available in the kitchen, but the cookware was lacking. He returned to Elisabeth.

"Hey, Elisabeth. You can make golems out of mud, so do you think you could make an earthenware pot?"

"Is that something you would ask of the person considering disposing of you? What a frightening fellow you are. Very well. What is this ursine-wear pot you speak of?"

With his limited linguistic talents, Kaito tried explaining what an earthenware pot was. Elisabeth snapped her fingers, a perplexed expression on her face. A moment later, soft footsteps echoed through the corridor.

The door to the dining room creaked open. Behind it was a small golem, composed of rectangular lumps of earth. It waved good-bye, then suddenly collapsed, leaving behind a pile of mud.

"Wh—? Hey wait, Elisabeth; what did you just do? Don't you feel bad for it?"

"Do not pity it. Contrary to what you may think, it possessed no will. Now, a pot, was it?"

The mud squirmed, eventually settling into the shape of a pot. Kaito followed up on his explanation, saying how it needed to be shorter and rounder and how it needed a hole to let out steam. The mud shifted again, and after a period of trial and error, it finally reached a shape Kaito recognized.

"That mud is quite heat tolerant. While I'm still unsure of what you intend to do with it, use it as you please."

"Thanks. That's a big help."

Taking great care not to drop it, Kaito returned to the kitchen with the pot. He filled it with water, then added the wheat and put it on the fire. By doing so, he could plug up the fine holes that had formed in the pot. Next, he heated some milk in a saucepan and melted sugar into it. Once it cooled, he added one whisked egg, then he stirred gently to avoid making bubbles. He greased the earthenware pot with butter, then scraped the egg mixture in with a clean towel. But this was where it got tricky. He had to put the lid on, then let it simmer for ten to fifteen minutes. He placed a net over the stove and laid the pot on top of it, but he had no faith in his ability to regulate the fire.

"So how am I going to...? Huh? Wait, this works?"

It appeared that the earthenware pot Elisabeth had made was incredibly heat tolerant. Even though the stove was blazing hot, the amount of heat the pot was receiving was the exact right temperature to simmer the mixture. The rest was up to luck.

Soon, a sweet aroma began wafting through the kitchen. To cool the pot down, Kaito carried it to the ice-spirit fridge. He let it cool for ten minutes, then brought it to the dining room.

To his surprise, Elisabeth was waiting for him patiently. She must not have had anything better to do.

"Hmm? Well, this is a surprise. I thought you'd make a run for it."

"Well, thanks to you, it turned out all right. See for yourself."

Kaito placed the earthenware pot before her. Elisabeth craned her neck inquisitively. She seemed to be waiting for him to remove the lid. Kaito grabbed the handle and did so, causing a sweet aroma to waft through the air. Upon seeing the pale-yellow substance contained within, Elisabeth cocked her head to the side.

"What is this? This is not pudding."

"Huh, they really were different, then. This here is *purin*. It's the version of 'pudding' I'm familiar with."

"*Purin*, you say. Hmm."

Parroting his word back at him, Elisabeth took a spoon and scooped out a mouthful. She frowned dubiously at it as it jiggled back and forth, then she put the spoon in her mouth. After a moment of silence, she took another spoonful.

"This is quite strange...or rather... Yes...it's so very...wobbly... and syrupy."

Elisabeth brought spoonful after spoonful to her mouth, eating with relentless vigor. In no time at all, the earthenware pot was empty. Her spoon clattered on the table.

"I approve!"

"I've been approved."

Elisabeth smiled, her expression gleaming with satisfaction, as if to tell him that he was capable of anything he set his mind to. For a moment, Kaito envisioned a pair of cat ears flopping atop her luxurious black hair.

For someone who's liable to torture others at the drop of a hat, she's surprisingly straightforward.

Just as those words creeped into Kaito's mind, Elisabeth snapped her fingers. Afraid that she'd seen through his thoughts, he braced himself for the Iron Chair to appear.

A chessboard made of red light glowed before him, no doubt magically conjured by Elisabeth. Seeing Kaito's eyes widen in surprise, Elisabeth spoke.

"It seems you're not entirely useless. In light of this, I shall impart unto you some information about your current situation."

Elisabeth waved a pale hand. The chessboard began spinning toward Kaito. As he leaned back, the board stopped, and her voice adopted a singsong tone.

"Rejoice, for knowledge is power. 'Tis the fate of ants and the ignorant to have their lives played with. 'Tis by obtaining knowledge that men surpass insects and become beasts, then become humans, and at times surpass even God."

Two large pieces appeared above the chessboard, one black, the other white. Both were adorned with wings. As they floated, Elisabeth pointed at them.

"In this world, God and Diablo are both very real. They exist in a higher realm, where human eyes cannot reach, but their existence has been proved by theologists, scholars, and mages. Of course, God and Diablo are no more than names we assigned them for the sake of convenience. We call the entity who created the world 'God' and that which destroys it 'Diablo.' Hence Diablo can only interfere with the world of man once God has abandoned it. But there is an exception. If Diablo has a contractor, all bets are off."

"A contractor?"

"Those who use their bodies as intermediaries to summon Diablo into our dimension, where it cannot normally exist, and form a contract with it. Diablo then fuses with them and corrupts their form, but in return they obtain power they can use as they wish. But summoning Diablo, who possesses enough power to destroy the entire world, is no small feat, and there is no one vessel that can contain it, so it has yet to manifest. However, even its fragments possess great power, and those exist in our world today."

The black piece shattered and began raining down upon the chessboard. It then changed into fourteen pieces, all lined up. Amid the crowd of pieces shaped like beasts and men, one wore a crown and was bound by chains.

"Fourteen people have formed contracts with fourteen demons. They are ranked—the Knight, the Governor, the Grand Governor, the Earl, the Grand Earl, the Duke, the Grand Duke, the Marquis, the Grand Marquis, the Monarch, the Grand Monarch, the King, the Grand King, and the Kaiser—and when people say 'demon,' they refer to these fourteen as well as their contractors. There are also their servants: those who pledge allegiance to them in exchange for a portion of their power."

In front of the fourteen strange-looking pieces now stood a row of pawns. As the fourteen placed their hands on the pawns' foreheads, the pawns, too, transformed into hideous monsters. Elisabeth grabbed one of them.

"The skinless knight you saw was a servant of the Knight.

Calling them 'demon's contractor's servants' is a mouthful, so we call them 'underlings.'"

Elisabeth placed the piece back on the board. The fourteen pieces and the grotesque pawns began marching.

"Demons derive their power from the lamentations of God's creations—especially from the suffering of humans. As such, the demons and their followers are responsible for no small number of disasters."

All at once, the chess pieces opened their mouths, which were filled with ugly, misshapen teeth. As a new row of pawns materialized, the pieces ran them down and consumed them. Elisabeth snapped her fingers. A piece shaped like a woman appeared on the board.

"The Church—a religious organization that worships an image of God that mankind once relied upon, a framework that guides people in accordance with God's will, and an institution created to preserve our world's long peace—has tasked me with hunting the thirteen demons excluding the Kaiser, who has already been captured. At the moment, my foe is the Knight."

Kaito watched as a piece astride a horse advanced in front of the rest. The twisted suit of armor atop a red piece charged toward him. The female piece turned to face it, wielding a glowing red sword.

"The Knight is the weakest of the fourteen. Yet, to a normal person, he would seem like a nightmare made flesh."

As she was speaking, the floor shook. Before the sword could reach the Knight, the board and pieces vanished.

Thud. Thud. The castle shook once more. Elisabeth rose to her feet, ever graceful. She ignored the baffled Kaito in her advance, her dress swaying with every step. Flustered, Kaito followed after her.

Elisabeth left the dining room and continued down the corridor. When she reached the door to the throne room, she cast it wide open.

The stench of blood and flesh hit them like a truck.

They could hear the barbaric sound of something gorging itself on meat.

After a brief hesitation, Kaito gazed through the hole in the wall. Atop the corpse of the skewered patchwork beast stood a new creature. It was gorging itself on the carrion, tearing away large chunks of flesh with its massive mouth. Embedded in its flank were human faces, each weeping as they ripped apart any meat they could reach. Kaito could hardly find his breath as he was absorbed in the horror of the spectacle.

Elisabeth turned and spoke with a wicked grin.

"This, too, is the work of a demon. I expected as much, but it seems a second has appeared."

"I can't believe you expected something like this..."

"The beast made it here without decomposing, so its materials likely came from the neighboring village. When a demon attacks a village, he leaves few survivors. But even if as many as a fifth of the villagers escaped, the first beast seemed much too small to be made of the remaining four-fifths. It's only natural to assume that another was forthcoming."

How can she make a prediction like that so calmly? Kaito's head swam as he pondered that insanity.

As he was thinking, the beast let out a scream.

"RAAAAAAAAAAAAAAAAAAAAAAAAAAAARGH!"

Then it leaped, its rows of breasts swaying this way and that. It dug its claws into the side of the castle. The entire castle shuddered, and dust fell from the ceiling. The beast turned its murderous eyes toward Elisabeth.

Looking up at the beast, whose head was protruding through the hole, Elisabeth sighed.

"Heavens. Even considering you all were dragged into this, it is a pitiable sight indeed."

"GRAAAAAAAAAAAAAAAAAAAAAAAAAARGH!"

"I shall grant you reprieve. Be at peace."

Elisabeth snapped her fingers. The ground shattered. Countless iron stakes ripped through the earth and stretched forward. One after another, they pierced the beast's chest. Even with its body torn to shreds, the beast still lunged forward, trying to catch Elisabeth in its maw. But its charge was impeded by over one thousand cold iron stakes.

In concert with the sound of stakes piercing their target again and again, a cloud of dust mixed with crimson flower petals billowed forth like a tempest. Once it cleared, the corpses of the two beasts lay side by side. Dark blood began pooling on the ground.

Elisabeth turned to face Kaito. A drop of blood painted her cheek, but she barely seemed to notice as she spoke.

"There may yet be traces of the Knight in that village. We're leaving. Attend to me."

Her dress fluttering, Elisabeth took off.
Reining in his trembling legs, Kaito followed after her.

✳

Elisabeth descended the stairs to the underground. Mysterious groans echoed throughout the corridor, evoking the sense of a labyrinth containing a monster. In fact, it wouldn't be surprising if there really was a monster down here.

She continued at an even pace, finally reaching a door at the end of a hall and kicking it open. Kaito stood beside Elisabeth as he glanced inside.

The room had no furniture or windows, and a massive magic circle was painted on the floor.

As he looked closely, he realized how intricate the design was. The air was thick with the rusting-iron scent of shed uterine lining. He then realized that the magic circle was painted in blood.

"A teleportation circle, etched in my own blood. It takes me wherever I please, as long as I can remember being there."

"Not a huge fan of the medium, but that does seem pretty convenient. We didn't have these back where I come from."

"Ah yes, you come from a world of machines. You would do well not to make light of magic. As my servant, even you could use your blood to summon something to your side."

"What, you want me to shed *this much blood*?"

"You should try it sometime."

"I humbly decline."

Kaito nervously stood next to Elisabeth atop the magic circle. She clicked her heels.

With a sound like a flare, crimson flower petals began dancing along the outer circumference of the circle. As they spun, so did their surroundings. The motes of red then melted together, eventually forming thick cylindrical walls. The smell of iron assailed Kaito's nostrils once more. In an instant, the flower petals had transformed into blood.

Elisabeth clicked her heels a second time and the walls of blood collapsed to the ground like stage curtains. The scenery the walls had been concealing came into view.

They stood over the remains of a battlefield.

That was the only way Kaito could describe the scene before him.

There was fire stretching as far as the eye could see, and countless corpses dotted the ground among the burning buildings. The only thing Kaito could think to compare it to was a photograph of a battlefield in a far-off country he'd seen long ago. Two hours had passed between the creation of the first beast and Kaito and Elisabeth's arrival, but the flames showed no signs of abating.

As he glanced over the burning corpses, Kaito could feel sweat trickling down his forehead while the stench of charred flesh filled his nostrils and the heat radiated across his skin.

There was a man whose top half was fully carbonized. An old woman with not only her head but her entire spine ripped out. A woman with her breasts cut off. A young boy whose face had been torn clean off. A half-dead child with their arms severed who had likely been trying to crawl away.

None of them retained so much as a shred of human dignity. All their deaths were gruesome. Unlike the beast, their corpses were comprehendible. That was precisely why the spectacle was so horrific, why the cruelty of it sank into one's brain. The urge to retch welled up in Kaito's throat before he finally managed to swallow it down.

There was no mistaking it. This was Hell.

This was a place filled with the worst things one could imagine.

"I mentioned it before, but this is a demon's doing."

Beside Kaito, who had lost the will to speak, Elisabeth whispered.

She stepped forward, then turned to face him, the fire at her back and her black hair dancing against the blazing breeze.

"Demons draw their power from the suffering of men, from the discord in their souls that suffering brings. This is the result. The methods used here are...cute, I suppose. Even now, much darker horrors are being produced elsewhere."

Kaito was taken aback by her words. He was used to pain and suffering. He was all too familiar with fear and with the unbelievable tragedies that occasionally befell people. But there was no way he could be okay with a spectacle as ghastly as this, with people being killed in a manner that lacked mercy or meaning.

"You call this *cute*? Quit screwing with me! No matter how you look at it, this is Hell!"

"Even Hell has its layers. And this is a shallow one. As far as I'm concerned, this might as well be a field of flowers. Demons give birth to much crueler tragedies than this... 'Tis why the Church left dealing with pigs like them to a sow such as myself."

"*ELISABEEEEEEEEEEEEEEEEEEEEEEEEEEEEEEEETH!*"

She was cut off by a furious scream. At that signal, a group of villagers emerged from behind a half-caved-in animal pen. The nervous men, clothes stained with soot, brandished farming implements as they surrounded Kaito and Elisabeth.

An armored knight atop a horse strode up beside them.

Kaito froze when he saw him.

However, the knight appeared to be a legitimate member of this world's armed forces. He wore a plumed helmet, and his horse and silver armor were adorned with a coat of arms in the shape of a lily.

There was a metallic *schwing* as the knight unsheathed his sword. Elisabeth sighed.

"Well, if it isn't a Royal Knight. I strung up those useless colossi, so what business have you with me?"

"Don't play dumb with me! I was dispatched to this village from the Capital, and I've been keeping an eye on you up in your castle. But now you finally show your true nature! I've known what you were all along. This horrible affair, all of it is your doing!"

"Are you dull? You gaze upon the Knight's work. Then again, I suppose those who've not witnessed it firsthand may have difficulty understanding it as such. Regardless, take care not to foist your incompetence on *my* shoulders. The Church has tasked me with hunting demons. I am not in a position to kill humans... for now."

"Silence your lying tongue! Who would believe such a tale?!"

The knight's voice grew harsh, and Kaito cringed. The knight pointed his sword at Elisabeth and spoke, his voice quivering with rage.

"Don't think that I've forgotten what you've done."

Elisabeth simply stood there, her face the picture of apathy, and made no attempt to refute the accusation. Her demeanor caused the knight to lose what little patience he had left. He fired off a frenzied account of her past deeds.

"You tortured the entire population of your fiefdom! You dismembered their bodies, ripped out their still-beating hearts, stitched every orifice in their bodies shut, carved into their bones, melted their flesh, gouged out their eyes, severed their tongues, and when you ran out of ideas, you killed parents and children, the elderly, and men and women alike! In the end, your sins reached even the nobles! Torture Princess! Elisabeth Le Fanu! Who would believe anything that came out of your filthy mouth?!"

Hearing those words, Kaito was reminded of the reality that had been thrust before his eyes a few days prior.

He recalled the scene he had witnessed as he died. He recalled the mountain of corpses, each without so much as a shred of human dignity. He recalled the bloodlust of the angry horde and the smile of the restrained girl.

Elisabeth was smiling even now, listening to the knight's tirade as one might listen to a small bird chirping.

"And I certainly haven't forgotten what I saw you do to my fellow knights at the Plain of Skewers! Do you have any idea how many sleepless nights I endured in the Kingdom after surviving that?"

The knight's sword hand trembled. However, he suddenly stopped talking and looked at Kaito. His armor clanged as he spoke to Kaito in a voice filled with confusion and sympathy.

"Why do you stand with such a demoness? I'd heard that Elisabeth was looking for a servant, but if she's holding you against your will, you can come to me. I'll protect you."

Kaito turned to look at Elisabeth. She crossed her arms and remained silent.

It was true that Kaito had been brought back to life against his will and made to serve her. And he'd personally witnessed her cruel deeds. In truth, he would like nothing more than to live a simple life of peace in this strange new world. Now was his chance to get away. But just as he was about to step forward, Kaito stopped.

"Come on, then. Hurry."

"Your offer sounds like a dream come true, but can I ask you a question first?"

"What is it?"

"*Why do you look at me with the eyes of someone who's just found their next meal?*"

After this question, an uncomfortable silence descended among them. The men, still clutching their farming implements, turned toward the knight. Some of them looked worried now. But the knight said nothing. Looking straight at the knight, Kaito continued.

"Back when I was alive, I met plenty of guys who would actually pass up a warm meal if it meant getting to beat up a kid. And you've got the same look in your eyes that they all did."

He received no answer. But beside Kaito, Elisabeth's shoulders began trembling. She broke out into laughter. She looked truly bizarre, her body twisting as she clutched her sides in amusement.

"Of course, of course. It makes perfect sense. Ah, but I didn't expect you to be a member of the Knight Corps. How laughable—say, would you allow me one question, proud sir?"

Her laugh was sweet. Some might even say it was innocent.

Her crimson eyes glittering with glee, she spoke in a soft, gentle voice.

"I slaughtered those five hundred men upon the Plain of Skewers. I slew them, annihilated them, *exterminated* them. And I certainly don't recall allowing a single one to escape."

Her smile vanished. Her eyes were full of contempt, and her question came in a voice as cold as ice.

"So why are you still alive?"

At that moment, the heads of the men wielding farm implements were blown off. The heads fell to the ground, their lips half-open in surprise. Swarms of flies poured out of their gaping neck holes. The flies then set to work dragging the bodies together with their tiny legs. They gnawed through flesh with their tiny mouths, binding the bodies' skin together with mucus and crafting a miniature version of the creature Kaito had seen from the castle.

Kaito stepped back, the bizarre spectacle once again robbing him of his breath. At the same time, the knight's entire body was wreathed in sapphire flames. His horse's skin paled under the light of the brilliant-blue blaze, and the rider himself swelled in size. In order to accommodate its wearer's unnatural growth, the rider's armor inflated like a water balloon. Long gray hair and a beard spilled out from the openings in the enlarged armor. The knight had grown old and hideous.

In the face of the imposing, demonic Knight, Elisabeth clicked her tongue, ever fearless.

"I know not if you were trying to lower my guard or simply consume my servant before my eyes, but in either case, you are a fool. If you had intended to transform all along, you could have done so from the beginning and spared us the childish farce. Your experience contracting with a demon and surviving the Plain of Skewers has taught you nothing, it seems."

Elisabeth heaved a sigh, then nodded in satisfaction.

"But perhaps that is why you failed to merge with any but the lowest rank, the Knight."

The Knight let out a furious roar. His pale horse broke into a sprint at a speed much faster than even that of his skinless underling. Fire and lightning billowed forth from around the Knight. He grabbed the blue lightning in his hand and transformed it into a massive lance, then he charged at Elisabeth.

She didn't dodge the blow, and the lance ran her through.

Kaito stifled a scream. The massive weapon gave off a thrumming noise as it speared through Elisabeth's chest. Red blood began dripping from the wound it made. The Knight then jerked the lance free and sent Elisabeth tumbling to the ground.

A memory flashed through Kaito's mind.

It was a recollection of himself, battered and thrown against the wall, then collapsing to the floor like garbage.

"Elisabe—"

Kaito ran toward her, then stopped. She was laughing. She twisted her stomach as she sat in a pool of her own blood and laughed, as if it was all so funny that she just couldn't help herself.

"Heh-heh, ha-ha, ha-ha-ha-ha-ha-ha, ahhh—ha-ha-ha-ha-ha...ha."

She grimaced in pain and rose to her feet. Kaito could see clear through the cavity in her chest. Some of her entrails sagged from the hole, but she simply wrapped the loose ends around her arm and wrenched them all the way out. Bleeding profusely now, she cast her guts aside.

"I see... So damage of this magnitude is about as mild as an itch. A far cry from having one's soul set ablaze. Now then, pay close attention. *This* is what true agony feels like."

Elisabeth lifted a hand in the air. A great cloud of darkness and scarlet flower petals spiraled around it. They then mantled her body, masking the hole with fresh black cloth. She grabbed something from within the huge spiral of crimson and shadow.

"Rejoice, half-wit. I draw this blade for thee."

She drew out a long sword. Its blade was bloodred, and it flickered with a sinister glint.

*   *   *

"Executioner's Sword of Frankenthal!"

She spoke its name, and the runes etched onto the sword sparked to life. As the light reached Kaito's eyes, he could feel the meanings of the runes forcing their way into his brain until the complete phrase made perfect sense.

You are free to act as you will. But pray that God shall be your salvation. For the beginning, the middle, and the end all lie in the palm of His hand.

"Come, let us enjoy ourselves to the fullest!"

Elisabeth swung the sword through empty space, as if she was tracing both her foes' arms. Silver chains flew through the air in tune with her slashes, wrapping around the Knight's forearms and wrenching him from his mount. He hung in the air, helpless to resist. A moment later, he snapped his fingers, and the beast drew up from behind Elisabeth. Without turning, she swung her blade again.

Chains wrapped around the beast, binding it firmly. There was a loud ripping noise as flesh was torn asunder. The shackles twined around its collapsing form and reinforced it as it took on the shape of a horse. They wrapped around the pale horse as well, acting as a pair of reins.

Elisabeth raised her blade to the heavens, and the tips of the infinite chains rattled as they spiraled toward the Knight. Once they were finished, the Knight's arms and legs were bound, and at the opposite ends of those tethers stood four horses, his own included. He called his steed, but the horse paid him no mind.

★   ★   ★

"Now, then...let's see how you like being *Drawn and Quartered*."

She swung her sword, and the horses set off in unison.

The Knight's limbs screeched, and his joints made popping noises as they were pulled out of place. His flesh, stretched to its limit, began to tear. Blood poured from the gaps in his armor. But the horses did not stop. The Knight cried out in pain and rage.

"*ELISABEEEEEEETH! ELISABEEEEEEETH!*"

His voice was brimming with agony and hatred.

The Knight drew near Elisabeth. Kaito, too, approached her from behind, then he gasped. The eyes beneath the helmet were human once more. They were different from when they'd been focused on Kaito and were now the purest blue. They glared at Elisabeth.

The Knight's contractor was quite young.

Looking down at the man's noble eyes, Elisabeth murmured tenderly.

"A survivor of the Plain of Skewers, hmm? It must have been painful. No doubt you detest me."

"*ELISA... ELISABEEETH...*"

"...My apologies, good sir. But the cries of a demon are as unpleasant as the squeals of a swine."

There was venom in her smile. The Knight roared, a sound rich with malice and bloodlust.

"*ELISABEEEEEEEEEEEEEEEEEEEEEEEEEEEETH!*"

The next moment, with the sound of meat being shredded, the Knight's limbs were ripped from his torso. The appendages bounced along the ground as they traveled, still tied to the horses. The fissure ran all the way up his abdomen, and his organs came spilling out in a gentle cascade. Beneath the helmet, the Knight vomited mouthful after mouthful of blood before breathing his last. Then his body erupted into silent blue flames.

"Let us return home. That *purin* of yours was delectable but made for poor sustenance. I'm famished."

Her sword transformed into a cloud of crimson petals, and Elisabeth walked off. Kaito couldn't help but stare. He thought back to the scene he'd witnessed when he was first summoned. That and the Knight's accusation. If he pried too deeply, he would invite nothing but pain. Still, he had to know.

"Hey, is everything he said true? Did you torture and kill all your subjects, then turn on the nobles?"

"Yes indeed. He spoke no falsehoods nor held any misunderstandings. Understand who it is you serve. I am the Torture Princess, Elisabeth Le Fanu. I have caused more pain and death than any before me. I was apprehended by the Church. And I am now tasked with slaughtering thirteen demons."

She answered without an ounce of hesitation. She was as ruthless and tactless as a demon, perhaps even more so. Recalling her feline smile from when she'd eaten the *purin*, Kaito almost felt betrayed. She was someone who hurt people, someone who took from others, and he made no effort to conceal the displeasure on his face. But Elisabeth followed her confession of guilt with something wholly unexpected.

"And once I've executed them all, I, too, shall be put to the stake."

Her statement was resolute. Kaito's eyes widened. Elisabeth stared straight back at him, her crimson eyes as clear as rubies. Her calm countenance gave no sign that she was lying.

A line from earlier echoed in Kaito's mind.

★   ★   ★

Until the day of your death, try to do some good at least.

So that's it. Kaito remained silent, perplexed, unsure of how to react to this revelation. Elisabeth paid Kaito a "humph" as she stepped onto the center of the teleportation circle.

"Once we return, do something about dinner. If you can prepare sweets of that caliber, surely you can craft a proper meal. And if you fail to make something decent, it's the Ducking Stool for you."

Kaito followed her but stopped for a moment and looked back.

The scene painted before him was an unmistakable hellscape. A scream rang out from far off, and the animal pen collapsed. The flames grew stronger yet. Thinking back on the Knight's bizarre form, he muttered to himself.

"...Twelve more of those, huh?"

Kaito lined up next to Elisabeth. She clicked her heels.

As the two of them vanished, the Knight's lance burst into blue flame, crumbled to ash, and scattered on the wind.

2
A
Hellish
Game

Fremd Torturchen

Having acclimated to his new world and strange situation, Kaito came to a number of realizations.

In order to maintain his soul's stability, the golem body Elisabeth had created for him automatically translated things into words he was familiar with. As a result, not only could he read and speak this world's language, but he could understand most of it as well. However, the translation didn't always follow strict rules.

Sometimes Elisabeth referred to things not by their names in this world's common tongue but in an archaic dialect. When Kaito heard this, his ears picked it up as a foreign language. Furthermore, there were many objects that had the same name as something he was familiar with yet were completely different.

For example, besides salt, pepper, and sugar, most of the spices in this world had completely different flavors and intensities than their counterparts from his world. When he'd tried to use them in the same fashion, the results had been disastrous.

"...and that's why my cooking is so bad."

"Ah, but that can hardly be the only reason. Your technique, too, is wretched."

Kaito made his appeal while his wrists were strung up in chains from the dining room ceiling like a prisoner. Elisabeth sat in an antique chair, the legs of which ended in clawed feet clutching orbs, shaking her head from side to side as if to say that Kaito was still at fault.

The remains of his grilled pork kidney with garden-fresh salad lay on the floor, skewered by a single sharp spike. If the chains holding him up lowered even a little, Kaito's right foot would meet the same fate.

It was a simple form of torture yet effective nonetheless. Kaito squirmed as he shouted his displeasure.

"Don't go giving me that disappointed face, dammit! You're the asshole who decides if I live or die! Cut it out, please; I'll do anything!"

"I can never tell if you're being rebellious or subservient... And you're far too useless. Your *purin* is the sole reason your torture is this light; if not for that, I'd have disposed of you a long time ago."

"Wait, you mean my *purin*'s the only thing keeping me alive?"

"Indeed. Give thanks to *purin*."

This news caused the color to drain from Kaito's face. Elisabeth nodded once she was sure Kaito understood his position.

It was then that Kaito realized. Even at the best of times, Elisabeth's attire functioned on a razor's edge. The leather belts wrapped around her breasts left little to the imagination. The height and angle from which he currently hung only exacerbated that fact.

From his current position, he had a clear view of the valley between them.

"Elisabeth— Er...um...Miss Elisabeth. I couldn't help but notice your outfit is a bit...risqué."

"Hmm? What are you saying? I— Oh...I see. Prepare to die!"

"You're the one practically showing off the goods! Blaming me for pointing that out is tyranny! Tyranny, I say! And hey, as far as my cooking is concerned, you said the dish I made after we got

back from the village with the Knight was good, too, didn't you? You know, the grilled liver, the one I cut up and skewered and added salt and pepper to!"

"In your mind, does that fall under the purview of 'cooking'?"

"Does it not?"

"No."

Elisabeth moved to snap her fingers. Kaito made puppy dog eyes, frantically trying to supplicate her, but she just laughed in his face. He braced for impact.

"Hmm? Well, if it isn't the Butcher."

"Hwah!"

Suddenly, Elisabeth released the chains binding Kaito's hands. Rather than pain, he had been prepared for death, but the spike vanished from his landing point. As he rubbed his back, Elisabeth rose elegantly and went to greet someone. Kaito turned toward the entrance and was startled by what he saw.

A man stood there, covered head to toe in black cloth and carrying a bloodstained sack. From the swaying openings in the man's outfit, Kaito could make out clawed hands and scaled legs.

Elisabeth cast her arms wide as she presented the man to Kaito, who had finally risen to his feet.

"'Tis poor form to discipline a servant in the presence of a guest. Give the Butcher your thanks, Kaito. Butcher, this is my dim-witted servant, the man who continues to disrespect your lovely meat."

"A pleasure, Mr. Dim-Witted Servant. I am your humble Butcher, friend of gourmands and vagabonds alike. I am grateful for Madam Elisabeth's continued patronage. I can procure any meat you desire, so long as it is 'meat.' I await your instruction."

"Ah... Uh, nice to meet you, too."

Kaito replied in kind, his face stiffening slightly. The Butcher's tone of voice was as unsettling as his appearance. Guessing at Kaito's thoughts, the Butcher scratched his cloth-laden cheek.

"Ah, well, it is true that I'm a bit mixed even for a demi-human and that my appearance makes it hard to tell what my primary lineage is. But I'm not that different from the fine demi-humans you're familiar with, so there's no need to be quite so alarmed."

"Demi-human... Uh, you mean like...the races from video games and stuff?"

"Ah, so your world didn't have demi-humans. Pay him no mind, Butcher. He hails from a different world. His soul is as lost as a soul can be. 'Tis best to leave lost children to their own devices."

"Understood. Then you may make the usual confirmation of the wares at your leisure."

The Butcher nodded, and as Elisabeth turned to face him, he pulled an assortment of fresh organs from his sack. He showed each to Elisabeth in succession and then returned them to the sack.

"Chicken and pigeon livers, pig intestines, as well as cow tongues and hearts. Assuming they meet your requirements, I can carry them to your ice-spirit fridge for you."

"Yes, good work. I leave it to you."

"So like you said, you really don't eat people, huh?"

"Perish the thought. Human flesh tastes terrible. Why should I pay exorbitant prices for something that isn't even worth eating?"

"Ah, so your hang-ups are *logistical*."

Kaito let out a sigh. The fact that human meat could be bought and sold in the first place was unsettling. But upon hearing his remark, the Butcher hopped up and down as he made his appeal.

"It is true that human meat is quite bitter and also true that it is an acquired taste, but there are many who find it quite enjoyable, you know. If you would like to try some, Sir Butler, it's relatively cheap at the moment. Perhaps it would open a new culinary door for you."

"Pretty sure that's not a door I should be opening."

"Oh, but are you certain?"

"Very."

"Very?"

"Hmm? Cheap, you say? I'd not heard of any battles in this region, so from where are you sourcing your corpses?"

"Ah, you see, there's a territory with a village graveyard and a castle-side river, both overflowing with human corpses. It pains me as a butcher to say that some bodies are recovered with the choice cuts already missing, but as for the rest, the acquisition is quite painless. Would you care for some? The ribs make succulent roasts."

Upon hearing this, Kaito and Elisabeth turned to look at each other. With a large number of partial corpses showing up, the two could easily deduce the culprit.

"Say, Butcher, does this not reek of a demon's doing?"

"Ah, well, I am but a butcher, so I care little but for the quality of the meat."

"I get it. You were so devoted to your interests that you ended up neglecting everything else. I met people like that when I was alive, too."

Kaito's eyes were half-closed as he spoke, and for some reason, the Butcher scratched his face like he was embarrassed.

In any case, after asking the Butcher the name of the territory, Kaito and Elisabeth set off.

✳

"To think that I would remember a town as remote as this. Marvel at my mental prowess!"

"More than anything, I'm surprised you had enough self-awareness to realize how out of place your usual outfit would be."

They'd teleported to a back alley of the aforementioned castle town, and Elisabeth held her hands at her sides as she praised herself. To Kaito's surprise, her outfit had transformed into a conventional dress.

Her slim waist was fixed in a corset, and her draping skirt was fashioned with a number of flamboyant ribbons. She wore her hair up and had even added a flower to complete the look.

Kaito almost wanted to call the combination of the snow-white dress and the only-pleasant-on-the-outside face a scam.

Elisabeth, who now presented the image of a lovely young lady, stuck out her chest proudly.

"Indeed, I am most sensible. As the demon has not made his appearance yet, I understand full well the necessity of an outfit that blends in with the common folk. Yet, for all the effort I have made to style myself as the innocent daughter of a nobleman, your butler uniform makes you look like quite the hoodlum. Hee-hee."

"Oh, shut up! If it's such a problem, just give me something better to wear... Hey, Elisabeth!"

Ignoring Kaito's complaints, Elisabeth walked on, heading out of the dark alleyway and nearing the main thoroughfare. Kaito hurried after her. Before long, he was struck by the wall of sound that was the unmistakable hustle and bustle of people going about their business, complete with barking merchants.

As he stepped out of the alley, Kaito found himself in the town of a foreign country.

While it was technically a foreign world, the vivid spectacle, the voices of the crowd, and the diverse aromas all reminded Kaito of the exotic land he'd once felt from the other side of a television screen long ago.

Turning to face the dumbfounded Kaito, Elisabeth twirled her decorative flower and grinned.

"And now, the line you've been waiting for. 'Welcome...to another world.'"

The people walking by had all manner of hair and eye colors: gold and blue, black and gray, red and green. A man wearing a shirt and a pair of suspenders passed a woman wearing a loose shawl. A girl wearing a dirndl was selling flowers, and a man wearing a frock coat smoked a pipe.

Lined up in the shops and stalls were various goods for sale, some familiar to Kaito but many unfamiliar. There was a semi-translucent potion vial with an artistic shape. A pink leaf with a saccharine aroma, packed with what looked like tobacco. An egg-shaped fruit being sold beside some apples.

A massive gong rang out, and a black-haired youth with lizard arms began ladling fried rice with pale-red lumps of meat to his line of hungry customers. While it looked tasty, it gave off a pungent odor, and most of the customers standing around eating it had dog ears and tails.

"Wait, lizard arms and dog ears?"

"Demi-human–beastfolk crossbreeds. Not an uncommon sight, particularly with the influx of various races in low-class towns. They make up about thirty percent of slum dwellers, and in the north, it exceeds forty percent. Visibly pure-blooded demi-humans and beastfolk are generally in the nobility, though, so they're rarely seen in human settlements. Get used to it already. 'Tis a bother for you to gawk at every little thing."

"Man...this really is another world, huh?"

"Oh, and the fruit samples aren't free, so do avoid taking them carelessly."

Flustered, Kaito drew back from the honey-pickled grape an old lady was offering to him. Elisabeth, on the other hand, plucked a juicy-looking berry and popped it in her mouth. She flipped a copper coin to the vendor.

She then continued making her way through the crowd. Amid the throng of hawkers calling out to passersby, customers haggling like their lives depended on it, and scraggly dogs and rats scurrying about underfoot, her luxurious snow-white dress stood out like the lone star against a midnight sky. But she seemed to pay that fact little mind. The crowd, too, passed her by.

"Hey, Elisabeth, where are you going?"

"You need not worry about it. Just keep quiet and follow me."

Kaito continued after her obediently. Just as he began worrying that she was wandering aimlessly, the nature of the buildings around them began to change.

There were no more shops, nor were there stand-up food carts or large-roofed stalls. What surrounded them now were shabby little huts. The nature of the products being sold became more illicit. It seemed that this area, far off from the main stretch, was where you could buy spoiled goods, illegal drugs, and weapons of various sorts.

Upon seeing a group of people slurping up some soup of dubious make between stone warehouses, Elisabeth stopped. When she did, Kaito overheard their comments.

★   ★   ★

"They say the Bloody Marquis is looking for employees again."

With a start, Kaito turned to look at the old gray-haired woman. She was talking with a group of friends, a box of medicinal herbs she'd no doubt been hawking sitting beside her.

"There isn't anyone who'd sell him kids anymore, right? They say a cannibal owns that castle."

"I hear Anna over from the corner did. Sold her fourth son for a silver coin, they say."

"Sounds like she drove a hard bargain, but even so, to sell your own child like that... Well, that's a whore for you. Betcha she gets a gold coin for her fifth."

"Better than tossing them in the brothel, I say. Word is that Marquis fella is even buying up the kids of bankrupt aristocrats to use as servants. I'll pass on being eaten, but if it's just changing bedpans, I could get behind that if it meant getting to drink *warm* soup for a change."

"The lady in charge of collecting people is supposed to come around in her carriage today. Heh, if only I were a bit younger..."

"You've got the looks of a monster, and you probably taste like one, too. Who'd pay any kind of coin for you?"

The younger of the two women laughed raucously, her long ears swaying and her yellowed teeth on full display.

Elisabeth nodded, then set off again. Hearing the sound of her high heels, the women looked her way with a start. Their gazes pierced Elisabeth like they were looking at something monstrous. Sensing their hostility, Kaito quickly chased after her white form.

"Wait up, Elisabeth. I wanna know where you're going."

"The corpses have been piling up, yet the town is not in a

panic. In short, the poor must comprise the bulk of the victims. After all, they have a tendency to drop dead on their own, be it from freezing, drowning, starving, or sickness. A few dozen of them going missing would hardly be grounds for a panic."

"You don't mince words, do you...?"

"Ha. Whether I mince them or spit them out, it changes nothing. I came to this district in search of information, and just as I suspected, a rather juicy tidbit came and landed on my plate. Though it would be convenient to have something more substantial... Ah."

Elisabeth stopped at the corner of the road. In front of the row of brick houses stood a black carriage. A well-dressed old woman who appeared to be its owner was grabbing the arm of another woman accompanied by a young girl and fervently arguing with her. The second woman wrenched her arm free, climbed a short set of stairs, and took refuge past the door at the top. The old woman clicked her tongue and walked back toward the carriage.

Before Kaito could stop Elisabeth, she dashed out in front of the old woman. Kaito had no idea what she was thinking.

"This is Lord Marquis's carriage, right? Oh, thank goodness! My name is Flora. I came from the main road because I heard you were looking for maids. I got into a fight with my father, who's a wealthy landowner, so I'm here in secret for a bit of fun. But I never thought I'd get this lucky! I want to live like a real lady. Would you be so kind as to take me and my servant to see the lord marquis?"

Kaito's eyes widened at the stupidity of it all. But Elisabeth just tilted her head to the side, her expression so pure that it made him want to ask who the hell she was and what she'd done with Elisabeth. The old woman responded with a hard, skeptical gaze. Elisabeth then gave a beautiful smile and continued without a care.

"Oh, I almost forgot. Back on the main road, Miss Anna told

me to tell you that she was the one who sent me. She's awfully nice."

Upon hearing this, the old woman smiled broadly and nodded. After asking Elisabeth the landowner's full name and whether or not her absence had gone noted, she cast open the carriage's door eagerly.

As she stood beside the sneering old lady, an even wickeder sneer found Elisabeth's face.

After leaving the town, the carriage passed a wheat field on its right before making its way along a riverside road. As it continued on, a castle came into view beside the narrow shore.

The castle was built out of an uneven mixture of gray stone and yellow sandstone and enclosed by black ramparts. The thick, heavy walls were supported by cylindrical steeples and stretched out far from east to west. The shadow it cast on the water was the very image of a massive crow, gazing into the river with its wings spread wide.

The carriage traversed the deep moat with the aid of a draw-bridge, then it arrived at the castle proper.

And so Kaito and Elisabeth reached the Bloody Marquis's castle.

✳

Perhaps corresponding to the tastes of its current lord, the castle's resplendent interior stood in stark contrast to its simple, ominous exterior. Chandeliers sparkled over the main hall's grand stair-well, and vast carpets of gold and silver thread lay across its floor. It was clear that each of the etched handrails on the stairs and plaster grapevines on the walls took no small amount of artistic prowess to create.

Every element of the house looked both elaborate and expensive.

Rich-people houses really are something else, thought Kaito with a squint. Following Elisabeth, he made his way across the hall and tried to cut through to the passage on his right. When he did, a large man forcefully grabbed his shoulder.

"You don't look like a noble. Servants go this way."

"Wait, hold up, Elisa— Mistress Flora!"

Kaito shouted as he was being dragged off. Elisabeth turned and gave him a thumbs-up. In other words, *Figure it out yourself. You're immortal, so do your best and don't lose. You're a clever boy, after all*, or something along those lines. Though he hated to admit it, Kaito was used to her attitude by now.

At this point, he didn't have much choice. His expression stiffened as he gave up and followed the man. Upon reaching the end of the passage on the left, the man raised a large flag with a coat of arms on it. The hidden door behind it opened, and the man prodded Kaito down a set of stairs leading underground. A sense of foreboding welled up within him. The feeling only got worse as he continued down the flame-lit stone corridor.

Finally, the man stopped before what was most definitely a prison.

"Get in."

"What, you're just gonna treat me like a prisoner out of nowhere?"

Kaito had been hoping for the ruse to last a bit longer. Unfortunately, his complaints were in vain as the man kicked him into the cell. A small scream could be heard coming from deeper inside. As he looked around the surprisingly spacious prison, he saw a crowd of young boys and girls, human and demi-human and beastfolk alike.

Their ages, genders, and races were varied, but the fear on each of their faces was evident. The scene was one of bitter nostalgia for Kaito, and he wasn't sure how to react. After agonizing over his options for a moment, he waved a hand to try to calm them down.

"H-hey, guys."

"Eep!"

Suddenly, a new prisoner was kicked into the prison. A young girl wearing a poppy-red dress bumped into Kaito and fell over. His quick reflexes allowed him to catch her before she hit the ground. Her chestnut eyes paired well with her curly brown hair, and they gazed up at Kaito in fear. Hers was a modest beauty, her plain features standing out against the diversity of the demi-human and beastfolk captives. Her cheeks reddened when she realized that Kaito was holding her, and she straightened herself out.

"My... My deepest apologies. My name is Melanie Eskrow, daughter of Earl Eskrow. Where...is this? My aunt sent me here to become a proper lady."

"I'm Kaito Sena... This is gonna sound kinda rude, but by any chance did your dad pass away and leave you in your aunt's care recently?"

"My, how did you know? Might you be an acquaintance of my aunt's, Sir Kaito?"

"Um, well, that's— Okay, y'know what? It feels mean to tell you this, but you're better off knowing. The situation we're in right now is super dangerous. I think you should prepare yourself to make a run for it if you see an opening. There's no telling what kind of horrible stuff is about to happen."

"Whatever do you—? Might I ask what's going on? What's going to happen to us and these children?"

"Beats me. I really don't know, but when people go into shock, they tend to freeze up. You should emotionally brace—"

"Get out there. You're being called."

Someone cut Kaito off, and the door swung open. A group of men led Kaito and the scared, sobbing children out of the prison. In order to keep them from resisting, they held a blade to Kaito's neck. A red-haired boy about his age and one of the younger kids received the same treatment. Kaito himself was immortal, but if he wasn't careful, the other two might wind up becoming victims. He clicked his tongue in frustration, then continued on without putting up a fight.

Eventually, the door at the end of the underground hallway came into view. It was made of wood marked with carved images of spiders and crows and lit on each side by a flaming brazier. The wood design featured the crows circling overhead as the spiders weaved webs to catch them underneath. It was in rather poor taste. The men threw open the double doors and kicked Kaito and the rest inside. Kaito expected the men to follow them in, but they simply stayed put and closed the door.

"Good luck."

Why do we need luck? As Kaito contemplated the ominous words of encouragement, he heard the click of the door locking.

When he turned around, his heart stopped in his throat.

Within the room, a bizarre spectacle spread out before him.

The ceiling was extremely high and domed like a cathedral. Its center was decorated with a floral piece of stained glass. But the intricate, kaleidoscopic light it cast was marred by the barbed wire lining the ceiling. The unsettling effect was exacerbated by the murder of crows perched on the wire. The crows watched over Kaito and the others in silent vigil.

What's the deal with all these crows? ...I've got a bad feeling about this.

Disgust and anxiety welling up within him, Kaito looked at the ground. The marble floor was cracked and missing pieces. Soil peeked out from the holes, and from the soil, massive trees grew.

Among other things, the room appeared to house a miniature forest. This, too, was an enigma.

Suppressing his unease, Kaito directed his attention to the middle of the room.

Atop a circular stage lay a rotund, snoring man dressed in a tailcoat. He awoke with a start, gradually rising to his feet as he scratched his plump behind. He looked at Kaito and the children. When he saw the man's face, Kaito was startled.

Covering the man's face was a bone-like white crow mask.

"Weeeeeeeeeeeelcome, boys and girls, to your very own Grand Guignol!"

The man's grating voice cracked as he shouted with over-the-top enthusiasm. Kaito broke out in a cold sweat. The man was cheerful, eerie, and *revolting*. Every instinct in Kaito's body screamed in fear, calling to his attention one fact.

This man was probably a demon.

There was no way Kaito could deal with him alone. But unfortunately, Elisabeth wasn't here.

"Whoa, hold up... You didn't tell me I'd get stuck with the real deal, Elisabeth."

"You all are the audience, you all are the scriptwriters, and you all are the actors. So I imploooore you: Enjoy yourselves to your heart's content. You may try to escape this annex, if you so desire. But only the last one standing will be saved, you seeEEeeeEee. Until then, I don't even mind if you all *thin out the numbers* on your owwwWwwwWWwn."

His voice cracked even more. Once he finished speaking, he fell back and collapsed. But before they'd had time to think about the meaning of his words, a single crow descended from the wire.

Kaito's eyes widened. The crow spread its wings as it swooped down, revealing a wingspan about the length of an adult man. It flew down to meet them. The wind pressure created by its wings was considerable, and, unable to endure it, Kaito had to close his eyes. When he did, he heard a scream from close by.

"No, no, *nooooooooooooooooooooooooooooooooo!*"

The boy in front of Kaito had been snatched up. Clutching the boy in its talons, the crow carried him up toward the roof. It then approached the arches at the sides of the ceiling. Focusing on the arches, Kaito could see spears sticking out of the wall.

But...why?

As if to answer Kaito's question, the crow impaled the boy on a spike.

Like a shrike skewering its prey, the bird gored the boy through the stomach and left him to hang from the ceiling. After letting out a gut-wrenching shriek, his body bent backward at a sharp angle and resembled a curled shrimp. He then started convulsing and coughing up a huge amount of foamy blood. All the while, his chest continued heaving.

Kaito lost his voice in shock.

He hadn't noticed them at first due to being distracted by the crows, but a number of children decorated the ceiling like lab specimens. They'd long since lost the will to scream. They simply writhed in agony, skewered alive in ceaseless torment.

Kaito felt a bead of sweat travel across his forehead. *My immortality means nothing here.* If he got trapped up there, he was done for.

A mass of crows took flight. The children froze in terror. Kaito screamed.

"Everyone! Ruuuuuuuuuuuuuuuuuuuun!"

As if his voice had broken a spell, the children all began moving at once.

Kaito knew that, like it or not, the curtain had risen on a fresh hell.

✳

Some of the children were wrestling with the door to the underground passage. But it was locked firmly.

"That's not going to work; just give it up and run!"

Kaito called out to the boy who was pounding on the door and sobbing, then he took off running with the rest of the children. Someone pushed Melanie, and she fell over. Amid the chaos, Kaito grabbed her pale hand.

"Melanie, this way!"

"Sir Kaito!"

"No, help! I want my mommy. I want my mooooooooo-oommy!"

A crow had seized the demi-human girl in front of Kaito by the shoulder. Acting fast, Kaito grabbed her leg as it dangled in midair. Her body stretched, and she waved her arms helplessly as snot and tears streamed from her face.

"Help, help, get it off me, it hurts, get it off me, don't let go, I want my mommy, I want my mommy!"

"Just hang in there!"

Kaito swung the girl's leg from side to side as hard as he could. The crow dug its talons in deep, and the girl let out a high-pitched scream. Then the crow collided with one of its neighbors, and just as Kaito had hoped, it released its hold on her.

"Rgh—"

Kaito barely managed to catch the falling demi-human girl, then he took off at a run alongside Melanie. His shoulder grew wet with the girl's tears. Around them, children were being snatched up one by one.

Fluttering black feathers filled his vision, and heartrending wails assaulted his ears. Droplets of blood rained from the ceiling to add to the chaos.

No matter how hard the children cried and screamed, nobody came to save them. They were left to drown in their hopelessness. His stomach churned, and Kaito felt like he was going to vomit. He spat a single word from the bottom of his heart.

"FUCK!"

With Melanie and the demi-human in tow, Kaito slipped into the forest's shade. Beneath the patchwork of trees, the branches afforded them temporary reprieve from the crows' line of sight.

It seemed the demon had placed the trees there to prolong the game. Revolting as it was, Kaito was thankful for that particular gimmick. After inspecting the wound on the sobbing demi-human girl's shoulder, Kaito turned to Melanie, who was sitting beside him, and ripped the hem of her dress with as much force as he could muster.

"I'm sorry, Melanie, but I'm going to need this!"

"S-sir Kaito, what exactly are you doing?"

"Bind her arm, would you? From here to here. I'm counting on you!"

"Ah, I—I see. I understand. I can do it!"

Clenching her fist, Melanie clumsily stopped the girl's bleeding. As she worked, Kaito peered among the gaps in the tree line to check on the crows. It seemed they hadn't noticed them yet. However, a group of crows grabbed another boy who was cutting through the middle of the room and carried him up to the spikes.

"Dammit..."

Averting his eyes from the horrifying spectacle, Kaito noticed something odd. Stuck in the trees were an ax and a sword, each with a cutesy ribbon tied around them. After a moment, he understood why they were there, and he felt the blood drain from his face.

"*Only the last one standing will be saved, you see. Until then, I don't even mind if you all* thin out the numbers *on your own,*" the demon had said.

In other words, the demon wanted them to kill one another.

"..This is so fucked up."

Kaito whispered to himself, his heart full of rage. At the same time, he felt as though a switch inside him had been flipped. What he felt now was the same as the peak anger, hatred, and fear he had felt at times in life, and they acted as a trigger to return him to a state of lucidity.

He looked at the weapons again and realized there was no need to let things play out the way the organizer had intended.

With these, he might even be able to turn this hopeless situation on its head.

"Hey, Melanie, can I ask you something?"

He called out to Melanie. When she turned to him, her eyes suddenly widened as her attention was captured by something behind him. A chill ran down Kaito's spine. Trusting his intuition, he dived forward.

As he did, he heard something slice through the air behind him.

"Hey, you're—"

"...!"

When Kaito turned around, he found himself staring at the red-haired boy his age, one of the other two who'd been at sword-point a bit earlier. The boy was trembling, and he was clutching a long sword in both hands. There was no telling what he'd do.

Kaito raised his hands in a gesture of peace, then slowly began talking to the boy.

"C'mon, settle down. Don't fall for the demon's—our enemy's plan that easily. Why would you believe what the bad guys tell you in a messed-up situation like this?"

"...*Sniff*... *Hic*."

"Is there any proof they'll actually rescue you if you're the last one left? Don't focus on killing the rest of us—focus on figuring out how to escape and call for help."

"Shut up! Nobody's coming to save us!"

The boy suddenly cried out in anger. He waved the sharp sword. Kaito raised his hands again and tried to pacify the boy.

"Settle down, okay? Settle down. Just take a deep breath. What makes you think that?"

"O-of course nobody's going to save us! My mom told me I

should just go die! She told me to die for the rest of the family's sake. She begged me to die. So why would anyone come to help me? Who the hell's going to save us?! And if that's the case... If that's the case, what other choice do I have?!"

"I see... So that's what's been driving you."

The boy was on the verge of tears as he spoke, and when Kaito heard his reasoning, he understood.

When a person believed there was only one path to survival, they'd take it by any means necessary. Unfortunately, such a path was often paved with regret. After deciding not to think and simply going along with the dirty work thrust upon him, Kaito had ended up getting strangled to death. He didn't think the boy would listen if he tried explaining that now, though.

Inching toward the weapons he'd seen earlier, Kaito forced himself to keep talking.

"So you've made up your mind and decided to kill me. But do I really look like I'd go down without a fight?"

"Shut up! With those fancy clothes you've got there, I bet you've been living on easy street up till now! Can't you just do me a favor and die? Consider it charity!"

"What kind of idiot would die for someone out of sympathy?! And if I'd been living on easy street, why the hell would I end up here?"

A little farther, and he'd be able to reach the weapon. But the boy had drawn near as well, and he brandished the sword with a warped look on his face. Just as the words *Oh no* passed through Kaito's mind, he heard the beating of wings.

—*Caw!*

A crow had seen them from the ceiling, and it swooped down. The boy let out a strange squeal and began waving his sword in a panic. Kaito slid past him, well aware of the danger, and grabbed the ax. Glancing between Kaito and the bird, the boy let out a scream of despair. The crow swooped toward the boy. Kaito raised his ax.

And with a *thunk*, Kaito cleaved the crow's head in two.

The crow fell to the ground. Kaito brought down the ax again and again. His foe was no normal crow. He had to make sure it was dead. If he didn't, he was likely to end up dead himself.

He hacked at its guts, knowing full well that it was overkill. Once finished, he turned to the boy, who was cowering in fear on the ground, and raised the bloody ax high.

"See, this is how we should be using these weapons."

The boy's face scrunched up, and tears began leaking from his eyes. Seeing that he was scaring the boy, Kaito quickly shook his head and lowered the ax.

"The thing is, uh, if we use this ax, we might be able to smash the lock on that door. And the underground passage is narrow, so the crows shouldn't be able to follow us easily. If we make it that far, we have a pretty decent shot at getting out alive. Leaving us these weapons in hopes that we'd kill one another was a big mistake. Let's show 'em that."

"...B-but I—"

"Well, don't just stay there all day quivering. Come on; get up. I'm not mad or anything."

After all, Kaito had already been killed once before. He could overlook a half-hearted attempt.

He extended his hand and motioned for the boy to get up. At his lighthearted gesture, the boy finally stopped shaking. Extending a tentative hand, the boy accepted Kaito's help.

*   *   *

And then, Kaito and the rest began their counterattack.

✳

Grabbing the arm of a beastfolk boy who had been hiding in the forest, a crow gave its wings a strong flap.

Kaito sidled up behind the crow, and as he jumped out in front of it, he hacked horizontally at its black wings in a single motion.

The crow fell to the ground with a muted *thud*, and the red-haired boy stabbed it a few times with his sword. Melanie hugged the crying beastfolk boy. Kaito wiped some sweat off his chin and looked over his shoulder.

"Is that everyone?"

Behind him stood the eight children they'd managed to gather while dashing from thicket to thicket. Kaito was disappointed at how few had survived. But he had no time to waste on shock.

The group had remained hidden by the shade of the trees and killed each of the crows with a single attack, so the main group of crows hadn't noticed anything unusual yet. Thinking their hunt over, the rest of the crows simply rested on the wire. Now was the group's chance to escape.

Kaito pulled a fresh ax and short sword from beneath a tree. The short sword looked easy to handle, so he gave it to the beastfolk boy before crouching down. He looked the rest of the group in the eyes, then whispered his instructions.

"Listen, we're going to make a run for the door. If the crows come after us, just stick to the plan and swing your weapons around like crazy. You don't have to kill them. Just make sure to keep yourselves safe. We're going to survive this. Now go!"

The children in tow, Kaito broke into a dash. The floor they had to cross held no cover, and it felt like it stretched on for eternity. Somehow they managed to cross it and finally closed the gap to the door.

Looking behind them, they saw the crows were in hot pursuit. Kaito swung his ax at the door.

"Remember, just do what he said. Spread out from there to there!"

The children fanned out in accordance with the red-haired boy's orders, then began swinging their weapons at the crows. Kaito knew this wouldn't buy much time. Ignoring the pain of the talons scratching at his shoulder, he repeatedly struck the doorknob with his ax. The lock went flying. Surrounded by a torrent of bird cries, he kicked open the door.

"It's open! We can—"

Just then, a scream rang out from behind him. He turned to look and saw a scimitar-wielding boy drop his weapon as a crow pecked at his eyes. The crow then grabbed the boy from behind and carried him up high. But the crow's sharp talons caused the boy's shirt to tear, and he fell. His tiny head burst like a melon as it collided with the ground. He died instantly.

His vision dyed red with rage, Kaito moved. Sparing no concern for his ragged arm muscles, he hefted his ax and threw it with all his might. The crow had moved on from the boy and made for the other children, but the ax caught it clean in the chest. It slammed into another crow and began spiraling to the ground. Kaito shouted:

"Run!"

The children responded to Kaito's scream and stampeded for the door. The red-haired boy followed after them.

As Kaito picked up the scimitar, he sunk the blade deep into another crow's head, then flung its corpse at the rest of the throng. They ascended to avoid the body, and Kaito used that opening to bolt through the door. He then grabbed the brazier from beside the door and threw it at the dead body. The flame spread easily. That should buy them a little more time.

The crows flapped their wings to evade the smoke, and Kaito returned through the door. Melanie and the children had already gone ahead. For some reason, though, the red-haired boy was waiting for him. Kaito blinked, then raised his voice.

"Hey, what are you waiting around for? Get a move on!"

"R-right!"

The red-haired boy started running alongside Kaito. The sound of crows cawing became distant. It seemed the fire had served as a potent deterrent. Kaito prayed that the crows would stay away.

The dark corridor was silent save for the echo of their footsteps. The red-haired boy spoke through the aftershocks of the event.

"My... My name is Neue. What's yours, mister?"

"I'm Kaito. Kaito Sena."

"Kaito Sena... I'm sorry, Kaito."

"What for?"

"I tried to kill you. I said that you'd been living on easy street."

"Don't worry about it. Anything I heard in that messed-up situation is already a distant memory."

"But you were so much calmer than the rest of us, and you saved us by killing those crows. You're amazing. How were you so bra—?"

Neue was suddenly silent. The two of them looked over their

shoulders. They could feel some kind of hideous presence behind them. There was a strange rustling noise, and they could see a black shape squirming around.

A vertical line of insect eyes emitted a sinister glow. Eight thick legs scratched at the rocky walls.

A massive spider was standing behind them.

Upon closer inspection, it was blanketed by a thick coat of crow feathers, and its mouth extended into a sharp beak. Kaito realized why the crows had stopped chasing them.

Being naive enough to think the fire served as any sort of diversion could very well have gotten them killed.

The crows had understood how disadvantaged they were in the narrow underground corridor and so coalesced, then they mutated into the spider now bearing down on them.

The spider spat out a thread. Kaito reflexively blocked with his scimitar. The very next moment, the scimitar went flying backward. It slammed into the spider, but the blade found no hold and simply slid along its thick feathers. The spider let out a frustrated roar and shot out more thread. Neue was right in the line of fire, and his face contorted in fear. Kaito saw some of his old self in that expression.

The boy in front of him had been ordered to die by his own parent, then cast into a desperate situation without an ounce of hope.

Unable to help himself, Kaito gave in. With a sigh, he *thrust out his left arm.*

The spider's thread wrapped around his wrist. Kaito immediately snatched Neue's sword from him. Based on its texture, the thread was likely as strong as steel. Giving up on cutting it, Kaito elected to instead *lop off his own hand*. With a dissatisfied cry, the spider reeled in the thread and began feasting on the hand with eerily non-insect movements.

The pain fired sparks through his brain. But Kaito was more than familiar with pain, and on top of that, his body was immortal. He could deal with this much. After all, if he didn't, he would die.

He returned the sword to Neue, then firmly applied pressure to his wrist as he started running again. Tears welled up in Neue's eyes as he ran beside him.

"Why would you do something like that? Why?! What reason did you have?!"

"Don't worry about it. I'm already dead."

"What?! Are you stupid or something?"

"Wow, rude. The thing is, I'm not originally from this world."

"What are you talking about?"

"Don't worry about it—just listen. My dad worked me to the bone back in my old world, and eventually he murdered me like I was little more than garbage. It was a pretty shitty life. Just when I thought it was all over, the Tortur—er, I guess you'd call her a sorcerer— She summoned me and shoved my soul into this fake body."

His tongue oddly loosened, Kaito found himself oversharing. The spider had finished eating Kaito's hand, bones and all, and it began shooting thread again. Neue brought the sword to his chest to protect himself. But this caused the sword to be wrapped in thread and snatched away by the spider. Seeing his face stiffen, Kaito sighed and made a decision. He didn't want to do this. But if it was the only card he had left to play, then he would play it. He took a deep breath, then gave Neue an order.

"I'm just some random dead guy. The next time the spider shoots its thread, you need to escape while it eats me."

"Again, what are you talking about?! You really are an idiot!"

"Again, rude. Sure, I'll die if it eats me completely, but it's not like I even wanted to be brought back to life in the first place. This is the end for me. If only one of us can survive, it should be the guy who hasn't died yet, right?"

Kaito looked at Neue, who suddenly seemed to him rather young. Neue looked back at him, his eyes watery with tears. This was the way to go. Kaito was satisfied that he was making the right choice.

Crying children didn't deserve to be in a place like this. And Kaito hadn't shed a single tear.

"You haven't died yet, so the world is your oyster. Good luck."

Kaito made his cheerful declaration. As the spider let out a hideous cry, Kaito bit his lip.

He really was afraid to die a second time. The fear he'd lost bubbled back up inside him. The pain of his desire to cling to life was unbearable. But he had no other choice. He exhaled softly.

He was going to die saving someone who reminded him of his old self.

And in doing so, he would become the kind of hero he had always hoped would save him.

If he thought about it that way, at least the absurd bonus chapter of his life would have a meaningful conclusion. As Kaito reflected on his decision with satisfaction, the spider shot its thread. He made no attempt to dodge. And then it happened.

"…Huh?"

Neue shoved Kaito aside with a *thud*.

The thread wrapped its way around Neue's slim back. Kaito looked up from the ground, dumbfounded. He stretched his hand out to Neue as a stupid question made its way across his lips.

"Wh-why?"

"Huh, I wonder."

Neue himself was unsure, and his voice was pure confusion. The spider reeled in the thread. The next moment, Neue's face froze up as he whispered.

"I guess...I was just hoping you could find happiness in this world."

Kaito swore under his breath. Neue gave a pained smile, and then he was taken.

A horrible scream rang out. Kaito scrambled to his feet. The spider could be heard tearing into something ravenously. Not wanting to understand what those sounds meant, Kaito charged at the spider. But as he heard the *crunch* of a collarbone being snapped, his thoughts were painted over with rage and hatred, returning him to a strange state of lucidity. He stopped, then muttered in a monotone.

"Ah......... I guess there's no use trying to save a dead man."

The next instant, he turned on his heel and ran. He was calm enough that it surprised even himself. His face was expressionless. But the fire in his eyes gradually roared to life. He voiced a single thought again and again, almost in a groan.

"I'm gonna kill that thing. I'm gonna kill that thing. I'm gonna crush it. I'm gonna kill it, kill it, kill it, kill it."

His voice dripping with bloodlust, he continued his retreat.

If the spider caught him here, Neue's sacrifice would have been for nothing. He wouldn't let Neue die in vain. That was the sole thought that propelled him as he ran.

The door at the other end of the passage eventually came into view. He'd expected the hidden door to be locked as well, so he'd given one of the older children an ax. After this much time had passed, they should have been able to break it down. Kaito narrowed his eyes. The door was completely unmarred. Maybe it hadn't been locked after all.

As doubts crossed his mind, the door swung open, and from it, a poppy-red dress appeared. Beyond the door stood Melanie. Calling in a sweet voice, she ran to him as fast as her legs could carry her.

"Sir Kaito!"

"Melanie?! Wait, don't come this way! You have to run!"

Ignoring his warnings, Melanie wrapped him in an embrace. She twined her soft arms around his neck. Her pink lips hung alongside his ear, and she let out a sweet breath as she started to whisper.

Before she could, though, the door burst open once more. A vivid color ran across Kaito's field of vision.

It was a dress far redder than Melanie's, a dress that had once been snow-white.

"Oh, if it isn't Kaito!"

The voice that rang out was so indifferent to the situation, it seemed out of place.

There stood Elisabeth, drenched in blood and energetically waving at him.

✳

"Why, I was just thinking of coming to meet you, so this turn of events is rather convenient. Quite sensible of you to come on your own... Oh? You're covered in blood, I see... And on the verge of dying from blood loss, by the looks of it. You seem to have dropped your hand somewhere. Was it the removable type? At any rate, I'd best bind the wound with chains...... Is that a bug? Ahhh! It most certainly is a bug! I despise bugs! Spiders are most unpleasant!"

Elisabeth jumped a little as she peered behind Kaito. As she landed, the ground around her feet burst with darkness and crimson flower petals. They spiraled toward the ceiling, then formed a large hole over the spider's head. A massive, thorn-laden weight appeared from the hole.

The weight whirred as it fell and then slammed down on the spider, crushing it.

"Squish it!"

Elisabeth raised a fist. Her attack was so ludicrous, it almost made Kaito want to complain.

She'd squished that terrifying spider as easily as one might squish a cockroach with a slipper. His wrist was now bound by a chain—a rather crude way to stop the blood loss—and he opened his mouth wide. Melanie clutched at his jacket as though in terror.

A heavy silence fell among them, which Elisabeth broke while tilting her head.

"So what happened here?"

At that moment, Kaito felt something inside him release.

Elisabeth's overwhelming strength, as well as her almost nostalgic carefree demeanor, allowed him to finally relax his nerves, which had been pushed to the limit.

He rattled off to Elisabeth everything that had happened.

"Oh, Elisabeth. There was a demon in the annex, and he was like, 'Welcome, boys and girls, to your very own Grand Guignol! You all are the audience, you all are the scriptwriters, and you all are the actors. So I implore you: Enjoy yourselves to your heart's content.' And then there were these crows…"

"Is that so, I see, ah, mm-hmm, is that so, oh."

Kaito was in a tizzy, and the words spilled from his mouth like a flood. He ended up including a number of unnecessary details. He couldn't tell if she was listening, as she simply nodded along with a dodgy expression and began walking before he'd even finished speaking. She held both hands behind her head as she walked through the doorway. Passing through the hall, she headed for the right-hand corridor. She then continued unabated, entering a passage marked for servants.

Embracing Melanie's quivering arms, Kaito followed after her.

"Elisabeth, are you listening to me? I said, the demon's in the ann—"

"Behold, Kaito!"

Elisabeth stopped in front of an open door. Looking inside, Kaito saw a kitchen.

Atop a cutting board was a noble-looking girl, her dainty dress stained in blood and her ribs savagely removed. Beside her lay a man with a bull's head wearing a chef's coat, his groin split in half by a saw. A demon's underling disguised as a chef. His death was no doubt Elisabeth's handiwork.

"Just as the Butcher said, the dead girl's body is missing some bits.

Apparently, those of noble bearing taste better than common folk. They dine on the nobles and play with the commoners. After playing with you and the rest of the common children, no doubt he intended to enjoy dinner up here in the main building. Ah, how luxurious."

Elisabeth nodded approvingly. Kaito clenched his fists. The rage and bloodlust within him had been validated once more. Oblivious to his fury, Elisabeth turned to Kaito and shrugged.

"The fools tried to eat me, and though killing them and making them divulge the location of that hidden door was entertaining, there were so many that some of them were able to flee into the courtyard. Chasing them down was quite the affair."

"Elisabeth, I understand why it took you so long to get to me. But I don't give a shit about that. We have to get to the annex. I need you to kill that demon for me."

"Oh-ho, well, aren't you fired up? Your wrist... Those who don't fear pain are few and far between. But Kaito...why is it that you possess the resolve to sever your own wrist and the experience of walking through that bloodbath, yet you are blind to the truth right before your very eyes?"

"What do you mean?"

Instead of responding to his question, Elisabeth began walking. She left the kitchen, made her way down the corridor, and stopped in the center of the main hall. All the nonunderling staff must have fled, because the castle was deathly silent.

Her dark hair swayed beneath the glimmering chandelier light as she looked back over her shoulder.

"It seems the demon here torments people not simply for power but because he enjoys it even more than our friend the Knight did. He takes pleasure in their pain and their screams. But aside from the Grand Guignol, it seems his interests run even deeper. So think. What is the most elaborate form of despair, the form that a twisted man like him would find the most delightful?"

Kaito had no idea what Elisabeth was talking about. But he suddenly recalled the time when his father was strangling him. He'd kept Kaito in a state of dehydration, then given him water. And just when Kaito thought he'd been saved, his father killed him.

The deepest form of despair was to think you'd found salvation only to have your hopes crushed right in front of you.

"...He gives people hope, and just when they think they've been saved, he snatches it away."

"Precisely! Once there are two left, and the only one left to kill before becoming the 'last one standing' is a frail little girl, any child would think that survival was well within their grasp—and naught could be more invigorating than killing them right then and there! Of course, your actions posed a flaw in that plan, but I imagine the demon had a good deal of fun nonetheless. *Nary a single child managed to escape, after all.*"

Understanding her answer, Kaito closed his eyes. The hall was silent. No children could be heard anywhere. Shaking his head, Kaito took a few steps away from Melanie, the sole survivor.

When they'd fled from that deadly game, *what monster's mouth had the children disappeared into?*

"And on that note, I doubt you enjoyed assuming such a frail form, even if only temporarily, however..."

Elisabeth smiled affectionately as she gazed as Melanie's face. But when she questioned the trembling girl, her voice was rife with contempt.

"...Why would an *earl's daughter* be selected as a plaything and not as an ingredient?"

★   ★   ★

At that, the poppy-red dress swelled up like a sarcoma. The sweet little girl's insides transformed into a mass of meat and cloth, and as her skin tore, it began leaking out like pus.

From within appeared a naked man with spider legs and strange white skin, his body covered in crow feathers.

The fat, bald man clacked his crow beak. After looking at the grotesque colossus and clucking her tongue at his spider legs, Elisabeth stroked her chin.

"The man downstairs is no doubt an underling or an imitator of some sort. So having lost your human form, you can even transform into a young girl, eh...? Although given that young boys were to be killed as well, perhaps you simply enjoy wearing girls' clothes. Ah, how unpleasant. And though you possess the human title of 'marquis,' the demon you fused with is none other than the Earl. And here I'd come expecting a decent fight."

"Who cares? Just kill that *thing* already."

"What's this, now? You've been acting rather oddly, haven't you? What, do you have a grudge or some such?"

"You're damn right—I'll do anything you ask. Just make his death as painful as possible."

Kaito repeated himself. Bloodlust bubbled up from deep within his heart.

His being the sole survivor was too cruel of a joke for him to handle. The Earl had killed the rest of the children. Kaito couldn't allow him to live. Even though he'd just been rescued, he wouldn't mind throwing his life away if it meant a chance to kill the Earl.

He couldn't bear letting him live.

"...Ha."

In place of a response, Elisabeth laughed. The next moment,

she kicked him, and when he fell over, she planted a foot firmly on his back. There was so much force in her foot, he was afraid his spine would snap.

"Rgh!"

"Do not think for a moment that you can give orders to your *master*, you cur. Your words do not change the fact that this man is *my* prey. With or without your request, I aim to make his life my plaything."

Elisabeth spoke coldly, then sent Kaito flying with a brutal kick to his stomach. As he landed near the wall, he spewed up a mixture of blood and vomit. Elisabeth turned to face the Earl.

"My servant's manners are lacking. But now, we can proceed without interruption."

She raised her arms majestically. The darkness and crimson petals swirled through the air, enveloping her body.

After the darkness dispersed and the petals fluttered to the floor, she was clad in her usual black bondage dress. Her slender fingers grasped the handle of the Executioner's Sword of Frankenthal.

Placing a hand over her half-exposed chest, she gave the Earl a noble bow and offered her own announcement.

"Welcome to my very own Grand Guignol. For *I* am the audience, *I* am the scriptwriter, and *I* am the actor. I have no intention of letting you enjoy yourself in the slightest. I shall make you squeal like a pig and writhe like a caterpillar."

After making her grandiose declaration, she swung her sword. Chains appeared out of thin air and traveled to savage the place the Earl had been a moment prior. But the Earl's eight spider legs allowed him to dodge them easily. He leaped back, felling chandeliers in his wake. He exerted his pale, naked body, and crow feathers began shooting forth from it. At the same time, he shot spider thread out of his mouth. Countless attacks rained down on Elisabeth.

"Ha! Too weak; too slow!"

Elisabeth ran about, nimbly avoiding the projectiles. The ceiling and floor became riddled with holes, but Elisabeth didn't have so much as a scratch on her. Even so, she didn't seem to have any openings to launch a counterattack. No new chains were summoned. Noticing this, the Earl laughed with a sneer, and his attacks surged like a wave.

He had yet to notice the darkness and crimson flower petals coalescing at his feet and above his head.

Suddenly, the floor and ceiling made loud *gong* noises and began squeezing him.

Or, to be more specific, the gargantuan, flat stones that burst out from them did.

The Earl was pressed between two large stone slabs. A golden rod that looked like a barrel organ's handle protruded from their center.

Kaito noticed Elisabeth sitting down by the pole's grip. She turned to the blinking Earl, who had yet to comprehend the situation he was in, and beamed at him.

"*The Wheel of Death.* I squished your familiar, you know—but you, perhaps, I'll take my time shaving down."

Grr, grr, grr. The round stones made an ominous noise as they began rotating. As she spun the handle, the slabs turned like wheels. One turned to the left, and the other turned right. The

Earl's body was being audibly scraped away. Feathers tore off in time with the rotating, and his pale, flabby flesh began to chafe. Blood, fat, and flesh began dripping onto the floor.

The Earl let out a bloodcurdling scream. His beak went flying across the room, and the human mouth it had been covering quivered in pain and fear. His earlobes tore, and his temporal muscles began being flattened. He cried out in desperation.

"E-E-E-ELISABETH, ELISABEEEEEEEETH!"

"What is it, O Earl? Ah, your voice is as unpleasant as a pig's squeal. Can you not retain a little of your dignity and have the decency to caw like a crow?"

"I—I can make you a deal! I can make you a deeeeeal!"

"Hmmmmmmmmmmmmmmmmmmmmmmmmmmmm?"

The wheels clicked as they came to a stop. Kaito's eyes burned fiercely, and his voice was low.

"...We're not going to take any deal you have to offer."

"I—I heard that when you finish hunting the thirteen demonsh, y-you'll be burned at the shtake. I-if you leave m-me alive, you, you won't have to die, either. Am I wrong? Our goalsh are in alignment. P-pleash don't kill me."

His face was caught by the sides, and the Earl's vertical mouth drooled spit and blood as he made his plea. Elisabeth muttered "I see" to herself, then she hopped down from the handle. She smiled sweetly to the unseemly creature between the wheels. Shivering in fear, the Earl pitifully returned her smile.

"You imbecile!"

Grind, grind, grind, grind, grind, grind, grind, grind, grind, grind, grind, grind.

With a sharp roar, the wheels began turning again. Waving his limbs frantically, the Earl let out an incomprehensible scream. But those arms were plucked from his sides, and his shoulders were shaved flat. He was crushed like a nut. The blood pooling on the ground grew more and more viscous.

Her eyes glowed with absolute coldness, and Elisabeth looked down at the man.

"Despots are killed, tyrants are hung, and slaughterers are slaughtered. Such is the way of the world. The demise of torturers should be garnished with their own screams as they sink to Hell with no chance for salvation. Only at such a time is a torturer's life truly complete. Yet, you tortured, not understanding that in the slightest? You embarrass yourself, Earl."

Elisabeth's voice was thick with hate and indignation. Kaito had never seen her display such bald-faced rage. With a loud *gong*, the two wheels finally lay on top of each other. Blood oozed from the crack between them. They'd finished crushing the Earl, and Elisabeth placed a foot on them as she murmured.

"You and I—we are fated to die, forsaken by all of creation."

She softly lifted her foot. As she did, the pool of blood transformed into black feathers. They whirled into the air, stopped for a moment, then drifted to the floor.

They fell silently and beautifully, like so many black snowflakes, and Kaito clenched his fists as he watched them.

"...Hey, what about the kids up on the spikes in the rafters? Weren't some of them still alive?"

"If they were, the Earl was merely keeping them alive with magic. They would have died along with him."

"...I see..."

"What's the matter? 'Tis much more preferable than an eternity of suffering."

Elisabeth sighed, seeming bored. Kaito looked at her in a daze. Once, Elisabeth had carried out the same atrocities the demons were conducting now. Yet, somehow, she seemed fundamentally different from them. At the very least, Kaito saw a large gulf between the two.

He stood up, ignoring the pain, and called out to her.

"Thanks for that, Elisabeth."

"Why thank me? I merely did with him as I pleased. To thank me for such an act surpasses buffoonery and strays into the realm of misunderstanding, does it not?"

"You're going to die after you kill the thirteen demons, right? But you killed him anyway."

"I care little about that. And I certainly didn't do it for you. After I've tormented the thirteen demons, or, in short, the last thirteen victims the Church has officially permitted me to torture, I shall think little of death. The people suffered many casualties to capture me, so if they desire my death, then burning alive is my duty."

She clicked her heels, then began walking. Her black dress fluttered as she spoke.

"Having lived the cruel and haughty life of a wolf, I shall die like a lowly sow."

Elisabeth grew distant. She muttered in a low voice.

"...For that is the choice I made."

Kaito, left alone, stared off into space. The black feathers caressed his face, as if grieving.

He thought of Neue and of the other dead children. He'd been the only one to survive. The end of their prison break was so tragic, it was almost laughable. But no matter how much he lamented it, reality cruelly refused to change.

Because he'd survived, he supposed there was something he needed to do.

Recalling Neue's last words, he spoke quietly to himself.

"Don't know how much luck I'm gonna have finding happiness in this world, though."

But he would do everything he could.

Clutching the stump of his wrist, he strode forth. As he did, one of the falling feathers burst into blue flame. One by one, the rest of the feathers followed suit.

Eventually, the blue flames took to the castle as well.

That place had been home to countless deaths. As the flames lapped at the stone walls, it almost seemed as though they were in mourning.

3

Treasury Hunt

The wild deer liver sauté with raisin marinade went flying across the room.

Kaito held up a silver tray to protect himself from the rain of food. He then skillfully blocked the knife that followed after it. It made a *clang* as it bounced off the tray.

"I. Keep. Telling you. Stop throwing the food!"

This manner of exchange had been going on for about two weeks now. He was more than used to it.

It alarmed him how acclimated he was.

At any rate, he finished blocking the attacks and fastened his gaze on the culprit. Elisabeth.

She had planted one foot on the table, and she was pressing down on her trembling brow with her index finger. The wineglass beside her that he'd so faithfully prepared was on its side. Magnificent tears welled up in her eyes as she shouted.

"It's vile! The sweetness and sourness of the raisin marinade… The liver that manages to fill the mouth with the taste of blood despite being dry as a bone… Both flavors combine so poorly, I'm convinced you have a gift for vile cuisine!"

"It is with great honor that I accept your compliment."

"That was no compliment!"

She threw her fork at him. In an impressive show of aim, the fork flew just a few inches above the tray and buried itself in Kaito's forehead. He yanked it out. Blood spurted from the wound.

"Miss Elisabeth, O Miss Elisabeth. I appear to be bleeding."

"Why should I care?! A servant of mine should be able to plug a hole of that severity with willpower alone."

"Not sure how far willpower's gonna get me."

Kaito pressed down on his wound and sighed. In truth, wounds of this caliber no longer fazed him. He'd been used to pain from the get-go, after all, and after having his lost hand replaced and reattached, he didn't sweat the little things anymore.

People really could get used to anything.

Yet even so, his cooking refused to improve.

When it came to food, Kaito's specialties were borderline nonexistent. Because of this, he simply couldn't come to terms with Elisabeth's incessant anger in the slightest.

At this point, he had more or less given up on trying to improve. Yet for some reason, Elisabeth still had expectations of him, and her disappointment seemed to grow by the day.

"I no longer harbor hope for your cooking. As such, you need not make dinner tonight."

It was after she'd sampled his second attempt at a salted, grilled heart that she'd moved to the throne room and finally given up on him. The clear blue sky peered through the crudely fashioned hole behind her.

The Knight's beast had smashed one of the walls, and she'd seen fit to simply leave it that way. Yet, she seemed to favor the room nonetheless, continuing to use it despite the damage.

She had repositioned the throne, though, and she rested her cheeks in her hands as she sat upon it. Her expression looked like she was harboring a headache as she turned to the waiting Kaito. She pointed to a door he was unfamiliar with.

"In exchange, I order you to spend today hunting through the Treasury."

"The Treasury?"

As Kaito parroted her words, Elisabeth stomped on the stone floor. In the middle of the room, a spiral of darkness and crimson flower petals flared up like a bonfire. It converged on a single point, engraving a blazing rectangle in the stone as it disappeared. It left behind a black door.

The door swung open from inside like clockwork.

Beyond the door lay a spiral staircase. Considering the layout of the castle, it seemed odd for a spiral staircase to be below the throne room, but given that he'd just seen a door appear out of thin air, he realized that voicing that particular thought would be rather foolish. He decided to be impressed.

"Huh, I didn't know the castle had a place like this."

"Indeed it does. A thought crossed my mind after the affair with the Earl the other day. Your cooking is worse than pig feed, but your *purin* is rather tasty, and your ability to stay rational under pressure and the fearlessness you regard me with are not without value. And when you air the sheets, your face flushes with amusing displeasure. In following, I have decided to grant you a weapon to use in the event you find yourself facing off against a demon on your own. You may select one item from the Treasury—whatever you deem useful. No matter what it may be, I shall grant it to you."

"Er... I guess I should say that I'm happy and grateful?"

"As an aside, the place I call the Treasury is, in truth, a magical space. I took everything that once resided in the castle in my hometown, moved it all here, and tossed it in. The objects down there have been steeped in hatred and bitter memories, so mind what you touch. Some of them *will* kill you."

"Wait, this is just another form of harassment!"

"Silence! Cease your whining and be off already!"

The kick that followed was both precise and accurate, and Kaito went flying like a toy ball. He was, once again, the very image of a cartoon character as he rolled through the door. With exquisite timing, the door slammed shut behind him. He tried pulling and pushing on it, but as he suspected, it didn't budge.

His path of retreat had been cut off. Surely even cruelty had to have its limits.

At the moment, the spiral staircase in front of him seemed to be commanding him to advance.

The rectangular steps hung floating at fixed intervals, gently curving their way below through the dim light. He looked down, but all he could see were steps going on seemingly forever. A tepid wind blew up from the depths. He couldn't even tell whether or not there was a floor beyond all those stairs.

"...You've gotta be kidding me."

Kaito reflexively grumbled as he peered down the series of stairs that had no railing to speak of. Despair began creeping into his heart. But he shook his head and reevaluated his situation.

Well, it's true that Elisabeth usually has a point to the things she says.

He would need a weapon if he was going to fight more demons. If he'd had one before, he might have been able to manage a better fight against the crows and the spider. And there was no guarantee he wouldn't end up in a similar situation again. He didn't want to make the same mistake a second time around.

*   *   *

Never again.

And if that meant hunting through this magical space, then so be it.

"I guess I don't have a choice."

Kaito faced the stairs, which could very well lead to the depths of Hell, and steeled himself. He spread his arms wide for balance. The *clack, clack* of his footsteps echoed against the darkness below as he began his descent.

✳

He'd expected the darkness surrounding him to continue on forever and was surprised to find that not to be the case.

As he walked, rubbish gradually began appearing beside the stairs. A massive birdcage and iron maiden appeared in the gloom, followed by a hanging rack and a wooden horse with no sense of rhyme or reason to their order. As the torture devices glowed faintly in the dark, it became apparent that each bore grisly traces of use. The iron maiden's chest was caked with dried blood, and the spikes sticking out of the birdcage were discolored with chunks of meat and fat.

Kaito realized something as he looked at the rusty tools. Unlike their magical counterparts that Elisabeth summoned, these were real. The ones Elisabeth conjured up were always unused. No doubt she had the ability to summon them without limit, each free of rust or fat.

So why is this place full of their mundane counterparts?

★   ★   ★

"Beats me."

Tilting his head in confusion, Kaito continued on.

He suddenly found that the stairs had disappeared and his path was flat again. As this space was throwing off his sense of balance, he had no idea when the change had occurred. The stone floor just looked like a larger step, and he continued down its seemingly endless span. The items around him became even more disorganized.

There was a gem the size of his fist, a round pot covered in three-dimensional bee ornaments, and a barrel of vintage rum. There was a tiger's pelt. There was ivory. A broken chandelier. Some kind of small mummy. There was a bronze ax, an iron sword, and a silver spear.

He pulled out the splendid-looking sword from the vase it rested in, then found himself stumbling backward.

"This one's no good; it's too heavy... And it looks like the ax and the spear are, too."

It seemed that the weapons the Earl had prepared were chosen such that children could easily wield them. However, the weapons in the Treasury were designed for hardened soldiers and knights. They didn't seem to offer any sort of magical assistance, either. As Kaito had never undergone any manner of training, he doubted he'd be able to use them to any degree of effectiveness.

He heaved the sword aside. It landed with a *clang*, then sunk into a pile of gold coins that resembled an ant-lion pit. Turning his eyes from the riches, he continued walking forward. But the farther he walked, the less weapon-like the objects around him became.

★   ★   ★

A comfortable-looking rocking chair. A sewed piece of embroidery. A painting of a deep forest.

"...Huh?"

Suddenly, Kaito's shoe hit something soft. He looked down and saw a teddy bear with cotton protruding from its chest. As he examined the space, he realized he was surrounded by children's toys.

Apparently, he'd reached the stratum containing items Elisabeth had owned in her early childhood.

As evidence that they'd been hers, the stuffed animals' chests were ripped open, and the dolls were all beheaded. The cross sections of wood, porcelain, and cotton were pitiful to look at.

"I guess she's been into that kinda thing for a while, huh."

Kaito muttered dejectedly. They say that people never change, but this wasn't adorable in the slightest. He almost flung the teddy bear away in his annoyance but, feeling sorry for it, gently set it back on its table.

As he was about to resume walking, a hollow voice rang out from far away.

"*Elisa......beth... Eli...sa...beth...... Sa......beth...*"

"Who's there?"

Kaito froze in his tracks. The next moment, a man's deep voice coiled around him like a serpent.

"*Elisabeth... Elisabeth... My darling daughter... Elisabeth... My—*"

The voice was incredibly creepy. It had the hollow quality of wind blowing through trees yet at the same time seemed almost hot as it coiled around his skin. Kaito felt that if he listened for too long, his eardrums—and eventually his brain—would dissolve.

"What...*is* that?"

Driven by an intense, visceral disgust, Kaito took a step back. The voice grew louder, as though it were pursuing him. Kaito broke into a run, instinctively trying to shake off the voice. But as if refusing to let him escape, the voice pursued him with strange tenacity.

"Elisabeth... Elisabeth... My darling daughter... Elisabeth... My—"

"Hey, what the hell is going on?"

No matter how far he got, the voice kept coming. He looked around for a way to escape, then spotted something. Behind the pile of broken toys, reminiscent of a mountain of corpses, was a door. It looked almost as though the toys were soldiers, protecting it. Willing to try anything, Kaito grabbed the knob and turned.

The door swung open, but behind it was not light but an even deeper darkness. After he passed through the door, Kaito felt his eyes widen.

He was standing in the middle of an unfamiliar room.

"...Huh?"

Dumbfounded, Kaito surveyed his surroundings. This was clearly a child's room.

The rectangular walls were covered with wallpaper adorned with a dull yellow floral design, and beside the window were cute confectionary-like plaster sculptures. The furniture was all white, and atop a beautiful chest of drawers with metal handles sat a group of dolls and stuffed animals. There was a four-poster bed, too, with pearl-gray sheets and a heavy mattress no doubt stuffed with down.

Sitting on the bed was a young girl wearing a negligee atop a pile of blankets.

Her chest was stained in the sticky red shade of blood.

★   ★   ★

She struck a gaunt figure, her wispy veins visible beneath her pale skin. Her long hair was no doubt once beautiful, but at the moment it was devoid of luster and the tips were all tangled together. While her round eyes and shapely nose seemed almost sculpted, those hollow eyes lacked anything resembling vitality. And her thin lips were stained with the ghastly remains of what appeared to be bloody vomit.

Upon seeing that familiar face darkened by the specter of death, Kaito gulped.

There was no mistaking it. This girl was Elisabeth's younger self.

Oh man... I definitely wasn't supposed to see this.

Realizing that, Kaito began backing away slowly. He continued doing so until he crossed the threshold of the door he had entered. Once he'd passed through completely, the scene in front of him shimmered like a bowl of still water that had been disturbed, and then it vanished. All that remained were the mountain of broken toys and the door in their midst.

It seemed that he had managed to escape the Nursery. Kaito looked around and breathed a sigh of relief after seeing the Treasury. But the haunting voice returned to assault his ears again. No time to process what he'd just seen, Kaito spun around and made a run for it. He ran with no rhyme or reason, desperately trying to flee from the phantom Elisabeth and the male voice incessantly calling for her.

Cut it out; cut it out... I didn't want to know about any of this!

Kaito had no desire to learn about that playful yet proud woman's past. And these were memories she'd likely rather not share, giving him all the more reason not to go peeking. He held little affection for her, yet he couldn't shake the feeling that he was committing an act of betrayal.

Elisabeth Le Fanu was both a proud wolf and a lowly sow.

The unflinching woman who'd introduced herself as such seemed completely different from that frail little girl.

Seeing her like that was not something for Kaito, as her servant, to do unbidden.

After running with that sole thought in mind, Kaito found himself in a new location, one with an entirely different ambiance.

"*Huff...huff, huff...* Where am I?"

Blocking Kaito's path was a tall stone wall. As he inspected it, he discovered that it was constructed rather oddly—out of tightly packed stone cubes. The wall stretched out in both directions. It seemed endless, as though he'd reached the edge of the world. Then Kaito noticed something.

"Wh-what's that?"

For some reason, a circular section of the wall was illuminated. Kaito approached it warily.

Iron shackles stuck out of the wall at the lit-up section.

Bound by them, like merchandise in a shop display, was a naked woman.

"What the hell?"

Kaito stood, stupefied. He had to look a few times to be certain of it. But sure enough, there was a beautiful silver-haired girl bound to the wall by her wrists. Her chest was ample, and her proportions were well balanced. Yet, she had been heartlessly cast aside.

For some reason, when Kaito looked at her, he felt like something was out of place. But in any case, he couldn't exactly keep staring at a naked woman. He would just as soon avoid being taken for a lecher.

Ignoring his conflicting feelings, Kaito looked away. He resorted to timid sidelong glances to confirm her condition. The silver-haired girl just sat there, unmoving, her head cast down.

"Hey, are you okay? Hello? Hey, you."

He tried talking to her, but she didn't reply. He had no way of knowing why she was imprisoned, and as such was at an impasse as to what to do. But given Elisabeth's personality, it seemed unlikely for her to take a demon prisoner. Kaito found it unlikely that this girl was an enemy.

And even if she was an enemy, at least he'd be the only one to fall victim.

Also, if he left, there was no guarantee he would ever be able to find his way back here. He would rather regret having saved her than regret not being able to.

With all that in mind, Kaito decided to undo her restraints. He checked nearby, but he didn't see anything that looked handy for that purpose. He did, however, notice a small leather bag tied around her ankle.

Her arms were bound, so she herself was unable to reach it. What a cruel placement.

Kaito took the bag and looked inside. He flipped it over, and out fell a key and a piece of parchment. Taking the key, he undid her handcuffs. Her arms slumped feebly to her sides. Even with her freedom restored, she didn't seem to have any intention of moving. As Kaito looked around for something to cover her with, his eyes chanced on the parchment still lying on the floor. Large red letters were written on its front.

INSTRUCTION MANUAL: WARNINGS FOR START-UP

As his golem functionalities deciphered the script, Kaito tilted his head. Suddenly considering a possibility, Kaito looked more closely at the girl's body.

As he did, he finally realized where his conflicting feelings had been coming from.

Upon closer inspection, he'd realized that the silver-haired girl's slender limbs were connected by spherical joints. And her straight silver hair wasn't, strictly speaking, hair but was made out of glittering silver thread.

She was a doll. She was probably just one more object being stored in the Treasury.

The next moment, the girl's head went *clack, clack, clack* as it began bobbing up and down. Her head swung to look at Kaito. Her eyes were made of emeralds, and they glinted ominously. Kaito was struck by fear as he returned her gaze.

Her face was as beautiful as a painting, but it bore no expression. And its surface was as rigid as a mask.

The girl's—or, rather, the automaton's—limbs began turning, each ball joint rotating in a different direction. Alarmed by the abnormality, Kaito ran his gaze over the parchment.

After reading the words in red, his eyes widened, and he started running.

★　★　★

Be careful, as it may attack humans during start-up.

Kaito fled with all his might.

From behind him, the sound of the doll rapidly crawling across the ground pursued him.

✳

Kaito ran, the Treasury acting as an obstacle course. He leaped over a chair, slipped between two chests of drawers, and slid down a mountain of gold coins. Finally, he reached his target.

The doll didn't appear to understand how to dodge, simply barreling in a straight line. As such, it took time for it to destroy things when it needed to clear its path. Taking advantage of this, Kaito created distance between the two of them as he fled. But he knew that if he so much as stumbled, he, too, would join the destroyed objects' ranks.

Hold up! C'mon! You can't be serious!

His leg muscles stretched near the point of snapping, he dashed up the final set of stairs. He ignored the pain, driving his body with sheer willpower. If he turned around, he was done for. He was out of objects to defend himself with.

Swallowing his fear, he somehow managed to reach the black door. But it was still sealed shut. He banged on the door, screaming in desperation.

"Elisabeth, open up! Open the door!"

"What now, Kaito? Have you finally learned your lesson? Henceforth, I hope you'll properly sample your cooking first."

"I knew you were trying to punish me! Forget that—just hurry!"

Suddenly, Kaito felt a chill, as though his heart had been pierced by a needle.

Trusting his instincts, he threw himself to the ground. The doll's leg pierced the air above his head. She struck like a serpent, attacking from a bizarre angle, and the tips of her toes demolished the thick door. Elisabeth's voice rang out in confusion.

"Wh-what now? What is that infernal racket?"

As he listened, Kaito dashed headfirst through the torrent of splinters. He was covered in wounds as he rolled into the throne room, but he was able to distance himself from the entrance to the Treasury. The doll staggered forth. Her gait and pale skin made her the very image of a revenant.

It seemed Elisabeth had gotten herself some wine, as she did a spit take. She wore a rare expression as her voice was alight with flustered fury.

"*You worm!* Just how far down did you slither?! That thing is an automaton, made in poor taste by my foster father! In the absence of orders, it simply destroys everything in its path! Why would you activate such a thing?!"

"I mean, I'm sorry for just turning it on, but how was I supposed to know?! I only took off its shackles, and it turned on by itself!"

"Taking off its shackles is *how* you turn it on, you imbecile!"

Elisabeth tossed aside her wineglass, as well as the round side table she'd taken out to pair with it. It seemed she'd been treating herself to a little rest and relaxation, but that tranquility had long been shattered.

"Ah, how vexing! To think that I should have to busy myself over a mere doll!"

She rose from her throne, irritated, and rapped her heel twice on the floor.

Darkness and crimson petals billowed across the floor like mist. A mass of thorns shot up from within it. But the doll's reflexes were superb, and her jumping power was like that of a beast. She leaped over the thorns, cleanly evading them. By clasping a thorn between her palms and the soles of her feet, she managed a landing that avoided injury entirely.

"My... To think you would dodge that."

Murmuring in admiration, Elisabeth held her hands behind her, then swung them forward. An iron ax made specially for decapitations launched from the darkness, flying over the thorns and aimed for the doll's neck. The doll's head, however, swung down, almost as though it had been dislocated, and just barely managed to evade the ax's blade. Elisabeth's eyes widened in surprise.

The doll's legs clicked as they bent, and she leaped again, this time landing directly before the throne. She closed in on Elisabeth. Elisabeth seemed to be timing her movements, though, and she snapped her fingers.

"Ducking Stool!"

A chair sprouted from the floor and cleanly scooped up the doll's behind. Leather belts strapped her into place. The Ducking Stool resembled the Iron Chair Kaito had once been made to sit in. However, its seat had no spike holes. In their place, long chains were affixed to the chair's back.

Suddenly, a rectangular section of floor around the doll disappeared. The space beneath her was filled to the brim with water, crimson flower petals floating on its surface.

With a grand *splash*, the doll was plunged underwater.

Perhaps the doll was struggling, because the water's surface bubbled and frothed. But after a period, she stopped moving. The chains rattled as they dragged the chair out of the water. The doll was still.

Water dripped from her silver hair. Elisabeth breathed a sigh of relief.

"Good heavens, at last it's quiet again. However, this thing can pump water off its body. No doubt it will resume function shortly. Perhaps it would be best to destroy it before it gets its gears turning again."

"Hey, wait a minute. Do you really have to destroy it?"

"I thought this was obvious, but failing to destroy it would be incredibly dangerous! Unless it was your intent that I spend the rest of my days evading a homicidal doll, that is. In that case, would you like to serve as my shield? Hmm?"

"No, I mean, it was my fault in the first place that it got turned on, after all... I would feel really bad if you had to destroy something so well made... Can't you just turn it off, like it was before?"

Kaito attempted to pacify Elisabeth. As terrifying as the automaton had been, he was to blame for turning her on in the first place. And he was reluctant to destroy something that had been so elaborately crafted to appear human. Not to mention how expensive the doll looked. He doubted his ability to make financial reparations.

"Hmm? One moment. As you say, it would be something of a waste. Perhaps we can make use of it after all."

As Elisabeth pondered, the doll began trembling before her.

An unpleasant squeaking noise rang out as the doll's head shook at an impossible angle.

Ominous light returned to her emerald eyes. Elisabeth then spoke quietly, almost in song.

"Halt, O gears, for thou art eternally fair."

The doll suddenly froze. The next moment, her entire body visibly relaxed. Seeing the doll transform at a few words, when Elisabeth had had so much trouble restraining her, startled Kaito quite a bit.

"Wh-what'd you just do?"

"An incantation to make it register a new master. Heh. For it to have worked means the doll's old settings have all been over-written. I should be able to set a new master for it now. In doing so, the new master's orders will take top priority. That should make it stop attacking people haphazardly. Now, then..."

Elisabeth made to open her mouth again. Before she could, the doll clicked her head into motion.

Clack, clack, clack. Distorting her neck, the doll looked at Kaito. He gave a small hop in surprise. However, the doll did nothing more but silently train her emerald-green eyes on him. Kaito looked back in bewilderment. Her gaze seemed almost entreating. Elisabeth gave a short whistle in admiration.

"Well, well, well... It seems to have made the choice for me. Count yourself fortunate. Apparently, after being saved by you twice over, it has taken a liking to you. Very well, then. You shall be its master. One problem remains, however."

"Me, its master? Wait, and there's a problem, too?"

"Upon becoming this thing's master, a 'relationship' must be established. Its creator had an unfortunate fondness for putting people on the spot, you see. Of the four relationships, namely: 'parent and child,' 'siblings,' 'master and servant,' and 'lovers'— only one is correct. Should one select incorrectly, the automaton will turn on its master and try to kill them. A trivial matter for me, but you would most certainly perish."

"One in four is pretty harsh odds. What should I do?"

"Oh heavens, I haven't the faintest idea. 'Twould be quickest simply to destroy it, but you seem to find that option distasteful. Ah, well, here... Among 'parent and child,' 'siblings,' 'master and servant,' and 'lovers,' select the one least likely to betray you."

Elisabeth smiled a devious smile, then resumed her position on the throne as if her work here was done. Picking up her wine-glass and side table, she leisurely turned around. Apparently, she planned on observing this as a detached spectator.

Elisabeth seemed to be set on simply enjoying herself. Kaito frantically racked his brain. After all, his life was on the line. He knew he would rather die than pick "parent." He didn't know much about siblings, but his memories of the one time he'd met a guy he was related to were thoroughly unpleasant. And after looking at Elisabeth and considering his relationship with her, "master and servant" was definitely out. Only one option remained.

"I guess I'll pick 'lovers.'"

"Well, there's a virgin for you."

A rude assertion. But before Kaito could protest Elisabeth's verbal abuse, the doll began shaking more violently than ever. Unable to withstand the convulsions, the belts restraining her popped off. Hot steam burst out of the openings in her ball joints.

Her response had been so severe that Kaito, despite himself, was more worried for the doll than for himself.

"Hey, uh, are you sure it's not broken?"

As he peered tentatively at the doll, her eyes snapped open. She tore off the Ducking Stool's leather belts, then leaped over the water tank and landed in front of Kaito.

Kaito braced himself for death, and the doll acted.

The doll knelt in front of Kaito, sinking to one knee.

"Huh?"

"I apologize for keeping you waiting. O my dearest, my darling, my destined one, my master! My one true love! O my eternal companion!"

The doll shouted, overcome with emotion. It was the first time he'd heard her voice, but it was oddly pleasant. She clasped his hand in hers and looked up at him.

Her face was surrounded by silken silver hair, and it wore the first expression Kaito had seen out of her.

Her emerald-green eyes drooped, becoming soft and viscous, and her white skin grew flush with blood. Her features were clean yet somehow amorous, and the expression on her sweet face was nothing short of enraptured.

She stroked Kaito's palm with her cheek in a deeply human display of affection. Her smooth skin was as warm and as soft as a human's. With an expression of absolute bliss, she whispered ecstatically.

"Henceforth, until the moment these limbs are plucked from me, and my head is removed, and my steel heart stops beating, I shall be your companion and your lover. I shall live only for your sake, and I shall break only for your sake. For whether you wish

to love me or destroy me, both privileges are now yours and yours alone."

She looked up into Kaito's eyes, then gave a small, bashful smile.

"By your own will, would you please cherish me until the end of time?"

Her words piled up like roaring waves, and Kaito and Elisabeth were as stiff as boards. Unconcerned with their reactions, the doll continued stroking Kaito's palm with her cheek. Her adorable actions were like those of a fawning puppy.

Eventually, Elisabeth whispered quietly.

"Um... Well, you seem to have pulled it off successfully. Are you...pleased?"

"...I dunno. This is a little..."

He felt that this was somewhat troublesome in its own way.

But after looking at the doll's blissful smile, he swallowed his words.

4

An Envoy from the Church

"This is delicious!"

Fork and knife in hand, Elisabeth burst into a smile.

It was the first time Kaito had seen her smile without even a shred of malice. The situation was so abnormal, he was getting goose bumps. It wasn't just her, either. It was the entire table.

The long table had been furnished with a stately arabesque tablecloth, and the empty seats were decorated with colorful flowers. The line of alternating gold and silver candlesticks was all lit, gently illuminating the silverware.

And the aroma of a number of elaborate dishes wafted up from the plates.

There was hog's-head jelly with brioche. There was a delectably sour salad with intestines, a bowl of lamb tripe minestrone, and a golden-brown kidney pie. And the main course was finished off with some foie gras terrine.

Finally, for dessert, there was a tart, topped with thin apple slices in the shape of a flower.

Elisabeth stuffed her cheeks with the freshly prepared dishes one after another. Large, exaggerated tears of joy welled up in her eyes.

"This is delicious, I say—truly sublime! True delicacies! You have my praise, doll!"

"For it to have met your tastes is an honor, Lady Elisabeth, master of Master Kaito."

The automaton stood at the ready by Elisabeth's side. Her emerald-green eyes gleamed kindly, and a gentle smile appeared on her face. Between her long, classical maid uniform and her adorable little maid cap, she gave the impression of having served in this castle for many years.

It was hard to believe that she was the same person who had been going on a rampage the day prior.

Although he was still somewhat afraid of her, Kaito asked her a question.

"So you don't just fight, but you can cook, too?"

"Indeed. In addition to combat data, my Self-Recording Device contains thousands of recipes, as well as many other useful skills. From cooking and cleaning to playing games and accompanying you at night, I can fulfill *any* of your desires, Master Kaito."

"Wait, wait, wait, wait, wait, you don't need to go that far. I don't need that kind of extra service."

Kaito waved his hands from side to side. Whenever he interacted with this doll, he often found himself at a loss. And whenever he did, the doll hung her shoulders with such dejection that he could practically see dog ears and a tail drooping from her head and waist.

"Is that so? Well, should you ever change your mind, please do not hesitate to instruct me as you see fit. I exist solely for your sake, Master Kaito, so no matter the time or place, doing *whatever* you want with me is my ultimate pleasure."

"Wait... 'No matter the place'...? You mean, like, outside?"

"Of course—outside is fine, too!"

"What in the world might you two be going on about?"

Munching on a huge slice of pie, Elisabeth raised her voice in exasperation. After enjoying the delicate blend of the sweet, crunchy crust and the gaminess of the meat, she finished eating.

She courteously wiped her mouth with her napkin, then turned to the doll as if to praise her.

"See, when my irredeemable butler booted you up, I thought I'd have little choice but to destroy the two of you together. But your aptitude for cooking proved quite splendid. Every cloud has its silver lining, they say. My congratulations, Kaito. Your life may yet continue."

"Geez, I had no idea I was on the verge of death for such a stupid reason."

"In short, you are saying that I was of use to Master Kaito? My deepest thanks. I can think of no greater honor, no greater joy!"

"But enough of that. You are a servant of mine. Nay, in respect to your desires, I wish to welcome you once more as a servant of my servant, but... Hey, Kaito. Give this thing a name."

"A name?"

"You would do well to stop being befuddled by contrivance. All things need names. And it is most inconvenient to be unable to call for your possessions."

"I mean... I wouldn't call her my *possession*. Even if she's a doll, she's still a girl."

Kaito shook his head vigorously. Owning something that was practically human was too big a responsibility for him. But the doll stepped forward, her fists balled up and her cheeks puffed out.

Curling her lovely lips into a pout, she pleaded with him.

"While it may be imprudent of me to say, I am most certainly your possession. Ever since the fateful moment you chose me as your lover, I have been your eternal lover, your faithful companion, your soldier, your weapon, your love outlet, and your sex doll. Come what may, I shall forever remain yours and yours alone. I beg you to remember that always."

"A-all right, I get it. Just try not to say stuff like that. But yeah, either way, it would be nice if you had a name. Uh…"

Kaito scrunched up his forehead as he thought it over. He fumbled through his memories for something to use as a reference. But he'd never so much as named an animal before. Also, he hadn't been allowed much social interaction. He could recall the names of a few of the women who had spent time with his father, but none who he had any desire to use as references. Even the woman who had made him *purin* had left in the end.

It was then Kaito recalled a soft, nuzzling sensation.

…Oh yeah…her. There was that one time. There was someone who loved me unconditionally.

A snow-white puppy floated up from the depths of his memories. She had belonged to one of his neighbors. She had become attached to him, and every time he visited, she would wag her tail and lick the tears off his face. He had been able to play with her for only a short period before he had to move again, but Kaito felt that was for the best. If his father had found out about his affection for the dog, he would have likely tried to kidnap and kill her.

She had been a good, kind girl. And her large, droopy eyes slightly resembled the doll's.

Despite some reservations, Kaito recalled the dog's name and spoke it aloud.

"'Hina'… How does 'Hina' sound?"

"It sounds incredibly arbitrary, much like you plucked it from a hat."

"Hey, I put a lot of thought into that!"

"You're brilliant, Master Kaito! It's the finest name in all of heaven and earth, surpassing that of any human, demi-human, beastfolk, mythical beast, or god! My deepest thanks! From now on, I shall bear the name Hina. Hina... Hina. I am Hina. The name that Master Kaito blessed me with... Hee-hee-hee-hee-hee."

Hina's shoulders began quivering oddly. She seemed to be happy, but her reaction was a bit frightening.

Just as Hina's christening was complete, the Butcher made his appearance. Elisabeth purchased a large quantity of organs from him, then handed it all to Hina. While she dealt with that, Kaito began piling the plates from the table into his arms.

Apparently, having a good cook around loosened Elisabeth's tongue. After bowing to Elisabeth, who was engaged in a lively conversation with the Butcher, Kaito and Hina headed for the kitchen.

Once they reached the kitchen, Kaito carried the dirty dishes to the sink. Hina, using the meat she'd received from the Butcher, began making preliminary preparations for dinner.

Watching her line up with utter certainty the jars of seasoning she would need, Kaito called out to her.

"So wait, you can tell which ones are which flavors?"

"Oh yes, I have registrations for most of the seasonings that exist in this world. I can also use their scent to analyze whether or not they've degraded over time and the minor changes in flavor resulting from the manufacturing process, so I can adjust the quantities I use as necessary."

"Wow. That's really impressive, Hina."

Kaito nodded in earnest admiration. Hina's cheeks went flush with embarrassment.

"I receive your praise with great honor. On a related note, um, Master Kaito, what kinds of dishes do you like?"

"…Uhhh, I don't really have preferences when it comes to food. As long as it's not rotten or poisoned, I'm pretty fine with whatever."

His eating habits in his previous life were more survival based, after all. He'd simply been grateful whenever he got his hands on something edible. Hina nodded earnestly in response to Kaito's half-hearted answer.

"I understand. Then I will give it my all to cook something you find delicious, Master Kaito. And then, perhaps—and this would be terribly august—were you to possibly find my cooking to your liking, Master Kaito… Ah, my heart would be so full with honor and pride that I would surely die!"

"Settle down there, Hina. Please don't die over something like that."

"Understood! Then I will live forever!"

Hina nodded, her cheeks still red. Vaguely muttering something to the effect of "by your side forever" and "Master Kaito," her body swayed from side to side. As he watched her plump breasts bob up and down, Kaito felt somewhat embarrassed. But he'd spent so much time alone in this claustrophobic dungeon of a kitchen, and now…

It really is nice to have someone to talk to.

Nodding, Kaito turned on the sink's faucet. The castle's water supply was linked to a reservoir full of undines. He was glad for the limitless source of water, even if it was sometimes annoying that it didn't come hot.

As he washed the dishes with cold water, Hina stood beside him, preparing the offal, her knife constantly moving. In the blink of an eye, the unnecessary sections were removed and the meat was cut to the perfect dimensions. As if to ensure that the meat not suffer more damage than necessary, the cuts were all clean and precise.

Kaito unwittingly stopped moving as he watched her masterful knife work. It was at that moment that Elisabeth's voice rang out.

"Butler! Oh, Butler!"

"…"

"Kaito!"

"I heard you. What do you want?"

Abandoning the wet dishes and leaving the rest to Hina, Kaito broke into a run.

He had expected her to be waiting in the throne room, but she was still in the dining room.

He opened the door and saw her sitting on her ball-and-claw chair, tipping a wineglass back and forth. She wore a sullen expression, and her legs were crossed. A new visitor sat before her, occupying the same seat the Butcher had been in when Kaito had left.

"Apparently, this unpleasant man has some matter he wishes to discuss with you."

"Ah, pleased to meet you… Young Kaito Sena, correct?"

The blond man's face was chiseled, and he wore a black cassock.

He evoked the image of a goat, and his eyes seemed gentle as he smiled. Yet, his face gave off a somewhat suspicious impression, and looking at him gave Kaito goose bumps on his back and an unpleasant feeling in his stomach. He also noticed that the man's pronunciation of his Japanese name had been smooth and more correct than he'd heard in some time.

Showing no signs as to whether or not he'd deduced Kaito's unease, the man opened his mouth with dignity.

"My name is Clueless Ray Faund. I come as an envoy from the Church, looking to conduct a personal interview with you."

".............Huh?"

"He truly is your servant, Elisabeth. His manner resembles yours."

The man spoke in a tone that made it impossible to tell if he was truly impressed or if he was being sarcastic. Kaito took another good long look at Clueless, the man from the Church.

Kaito didn't know much about this world's Church. But based on the fact that they'd been able to suspend Elisabeth's execution and order her on her demon hunt, he could tell they wielded substantial influence. In the face of such power, Kaito's first reaction was the desire to flee. But if he fled now, it would look highly suspicious. Suppressing his automatic response, which was to turn around, Kaito focused his gaze on the man, silently inquiring as to what questions he wanted to ask.

Clueless stood from his chair, stretched, and offered a rather unexpected proposal.

"Well then, shall we make our way to the Church? I'd rather not hear you out in a place as gloomy as this castle."

"Huh? Well-I'm-Lady-Elisabeth's-butler-you-see. I can't just come and go as I please."

"Insolent cur... So you'll admit to being my servant when it's convenient for you, I see. Nevertheless, he speaks the truth, Clueless. Do not simply carry off my servants with you. I made that one myself. The core component may be worthless, but it comes attached to a rather splendid golem, so he ends up being somewhat useful. You shan't take him without my permission."

"You say that, Elisabeth. But you're the one who failed to report having summoned the soul of someone from another world, aren't you?"

At Clueless's declaration, Elisabeth twisted her lips. He seemed to have hit the mark. Kaito was fairly surprised that the fact that he was from another world had been exposed.

Laying his large hands one on top of the other, Clueless continued.

"However, I have no intention of reporting that fact to my superiors. I can say that I simply wanted to check on the specifics of how you defeated the Knight and the Earl, and besides, this little visit was off the books in the first place. Don't you think that rather than dealing with formalities and punishments, it would be more constructive to quietly resolve this matter together? To that end, I would like to speak with the young man. How does that sound?"

"Bah, enough with the farce. At any rate, you intend to blather on and grumble until I relinquish him to you, am I wrong? Fine, then. What a bother. You have my permission. If you fail to return him, however, I shall have your head."

"There's a good girl, Elisabeth. A most sensible choice indeed."

Watching their exchange, Kaito couldn't help but be surprised.

He hadn't thought there was a person alive who could stand up to Elisabeth the way Clueless just did. Nodding to Kaito, Clueless began walking.

From the way the conversation had gone, Kaito guessed he was supposed to follow.

Neither party seemed to have the slightest interest in how he felt.

Half-desperate, Kaito obediently followed after the cassock-clad man. He accompanied Clueless down an underground passage, and they arrived at Elisabeth's teleportation circle. Kaito, having thought they'd been heading outside, knit his brows. Clueless stood in front of the circle and turned to look at Kaito.

"Now then, young Kaito, shall we be off? Do mind the vertigo."

Clueless reached inside his cassock and pulled out a heavy-looking silver pendant. At the end of its thick chain hung an upside-down sculpture of a veiled woman. The intricately carved veil defied gravity in its obstinate quest to conceal the woman's face.

"Guide me down the path of righteousness."

He held it over the center of the circle, and the bloody runes blurred. Crimson drops began pouring into the air. They then glowed blue and began orbiting like little planets. When the rotations reached their peak speed, the blue lights froze. They then fell to the floor as one.

When the blue rain had cleared up, a basement with a notably different ambience to the one they were in before spread out before them.

"This place is…"

Apparently, they'd reached a place separate from Elisabeth's basement. The walls were made of bare packed earth, giving off a completely different sense of claustrophobia than stone. The cool air had a damp odor, announcing loud and clear that they were underground.

"Come now, young Kaito—follow me. We're going this way."

Placing his pendant back in his cassock, Clueless left through the single door.

Outside the room, long, tunnel-like wooden passages extended to both sides. Old magical lanterns hung from the low ceiling and lit the path. It felt almost like a passage built for mining.

As he walked through the corridor rich in smells of soil and rotting wood, Clueless spoke quietly.

"These are the hidden passageways that extend beneath the Church. They connect to my private chamber. Follow me."

Obeying the instructions, Kaito turned halfway through the passage and made his way up a narrow staircase.

Beyond it was a surprisingly small room. Its wooden interior was barren, save for a stately desk and a filing cabinet. One wall, however, was adorned with an image of the same inverted, veiled woman Kaito had just seen. Upon closer inspection, he saw a single red tear running down the woman's cheek.

Ignoring Kaito, Clueless knelt and offered a heartfelt prayer to the woman. After a few moments, he stood back up.

"Forgive me for the wait. And please make yourself comfortable."

"Ah, thanks."

Kaito, being offered the chair at the desk, took it. While he did, Clueless busied himself with the porcelain tea set that had been left on the desk. He poured a pinkish liquid into a cup. A surprisingly refreshing minty aroma wafted up from it.

"I'm quite a fan of this tea, you see. I buy it up every time I'm at my favorite shop."

"Uh... Ah, well, that seems like a pleasant hobby."

"Ha-ha, I wonder. I'm glad you think so, at least. My subordinates often scold me for buying too much."

Clueless winked. It was a very human gesture, but for whatever reason, it made Kaito tense up. Something about the way the man talked seemed uncanny, almost superficial.

Clueless moved his own chair such that he was facing Kaito from across the desk. Kaito noted that the arrangement resembled an interrogation. Clueless took a sip of his tea, then began the conversation in earnest.

"I must say, I never imagined Elisabeth would drag someone from another world into her demon hunt, even if only as a servant."

"Uh, not that Elisabeth really talks about it much, but I got the vibe that it wasn't really a big deal. Are you saying it's uncommon for people to get summoned from other worlds?"

"Wait, she hasn't bothered explaining anything? Well, she's never been much of a responsible one. *Uncommon* would be putting it lightly. It's beyond rare. I'd heard the two of you had shared some memories during the summons, but you and Elisabeth must really be on the same wavelength. That, or perhaps you have similar natures."

"You're saying I'm similar to that woman?"

Kaito immediately frowned. He would hardly describe himself as similar to that proud, haughty, devil-may-care woman. Taking another sip of tea, Clueless shook his head.

"I'm sorry; that was rude of me. I certainly don't find the two of you similar. After all, I've heard that Elisabeth Le Fanu's cruelty started quite early on in her childhood."

The statement caused Kaito to start. The image of the young girl he'd seen a few days prior flashed through his mind.

She'd just sat on her bed, her body thin and frail and her eyes hollow.

Kaito shook his head to dispel the vision. Ignoring Kaito's unrest, Clueless continued on.

"She was born as the only child of the distinguished Le Fanu family. She was a feeble child who broke toys and delighted at the deaths of animals, but she didn't truly bloom until she turned sixteen. It was at that point that she began torturing people, gaining significant magical ability from their pain. And with those wicked powers, she killed even more. As she committed her many, *many* atrocities, no entity, living or dead, could inspire fear in her any longer, least of all God."

Clueless's hand squeezed down on his porcelain cup. A stern light burned in his azure eyes, and Kaito could tell that his voice was full of needle-sharp hostility. Clueless had been chatting merrily with Elisabeth just a moment ago, but his words were now steeped in hatred.

Squinting in the face of the severity of Clueless's reaction, a seed of doubt took root in Kaito's mind.

Obtaining power from the pain of others—that was exactly what the demons did. But Elisabeth Le Fanu was no demon; she was the Torture Princess.

"I thought Elisabeth wasn't one of the fourteen demons, though?"

"True, she isn't. She accomplished that all by herself, not contracting with anyone or anything. She shouldn't be able to use the powers of demons, and none but the High Priest has been able to discern the mechanism by which she's able to turn people's pain into her own power. But the facts are the facts. She is an evil woman, with powers surpassing those of the demons. Her very existence is blasphemous."

Clueless spat these words. Perhaps he was right, but Kaito wasn't sure how to respond. It was true that Elisabeth was a torturer, a despot, and a tyrant. But now, she was fighting the demons. And the number of people in this world who could stand up to those hell-birthing monsters probably wasn't high.

And for now, Kaito was assisting her.

While he still lashed back at her at times, ever since the incident with the Earl, he'd stopped having qualms about serving her. He even kind of liked the innocent side she occasionally revealed.

Maybe it was a warped way to live, but it worked for him.

In his hesitation, Kaito had grown silent. But Clueless nodded, seeming to understand Kaito's position, and heaved a heavy sigh.

"Forgive me. It appears I have gotten rather heated. But I thought that you, after spending some time with her, would find such things obvious. Now then, would you mind if I asked a few questions about your world? I hear that your world is where machines have progressed further than magic has; is that correct?"

"Huh? Oh, yeah. Or rather, magic doesn't really exist in my world at all... At least as far as I know."

Kaito matter-of-factly answered Clueless's questions. But on top of the fact that his knowledge of his previous world was strongly biased, he knew nothing about the workings of many of the industrial technologies he had benefitted from in life. But even though their exchange touched only on broad generalities, Clueless appeared enraptured.

He finished his tea, then gently shook his head.

"Thank you. I learned quite a bit. And you have my

condolences. The battle against the demons will no doubt grow fiercer from here. I find it difficult to imagine you continuing to serve Elisabeth once she finishes killing all thirteen demons."

"Is... Is that so? I mean, this body is immortal, but I expect it'll get pretty rough from here."

"Quite. And even on the off chance you do survive, all that awaits you is an inquisition by the Church."

"Wait, what?"

Kaito raised his voice in surprise. Clueless was unbothered by his rudeness. As he stared at Kaito, something resembling sentimentality welled up in his blue eyes.

However, it wasn't the gaze of one looking at another human but of one looking down at a worm.

"Why so surprised? It's a natural measure to take, no? The Church can't exactly allow one of Elisabeth's puppets to roam free after she completes her task. The stake awaits you both. At best, you'll be confined, but not before being thoroughly tortured."

"That's... Okay, I'm gonna be honest with you. I'd rather pass. I got sucked into this mess against my will. You guys are the ones in charge of the torture, right? Can't you do something about that?"

"It just so happens that I have a proposal for you."

Clueless leaned forward in his seat. As he did, Kaito felt as though a piece of the incongruous puzzle he'd been a part of had finally slid into place. All the talk leading up to this had been a mere prelude. Clueless appeared attentive, but Kaito got the sense that it had all gone in one ear and out the other.

"Think about this. I consider Elisabeth dangerous enough that I've been unofficially monitoring her as well as occasionally dropping by to check up on her. After the Church captured her, we bound her in such a way that she could not resist us or try to escape. But if she was to form a contract with one of the thirteen demons, her power would grow, and those shackles would be insufficient to restrain her. In fact, if her unique power was to synergize with the demon's, it would be quite terrifying indeed."

"Are you sure you should be making someone like that fight for you?"

"She swore she wouldn't forge a contract with a demon, and the head of the Church, Godot Deus, told us to believe in that promise. He also said that should the time come when she breaks that promise, he would sacrifice his life and soul to seal her away... But while he likely possesses the power to make good on his word, we would still be losing the most distinguished member of our clergy. Having anticipated such a calamity, I cannot, in good faith, sit idly by and allow the birth of a demon that will surpass all demons."

Clueless reached inside his cassock and once more withdrew the pendant with the upside-down suffering woman. He carefully opened its hidden compartment and pulled out a vial.

He tilted it over Kaito's cup, and a single tear-like drop of clear, colorless liquid made ripples in his tea. As it did, it briefly stained the pinkish tea deep purple. The tea quickly returned to its original color.

"If you make Elisabeth drink this poison, I can promise you a painless death."

"You're promising me death?"

"That I am. Your existence is an affront to God, and I cannot permit it to continue. Although from what I heard, upon being summoned, you wished to die anyway, correct? Having served under her, you know how terrifying pain can be. Do you understand what I'm offering you? I myself think the terms are rather fair."

Clueless smiled. Remembering the uncomfortable feeling he'd initially been getting from the man, Kaito felt validated once more. Clueless was arrogant. He seemed to be looking down on Kaito from so high up that he didn't even realize he was being arrogant.

Clueless no doubt thought he was being earnestly merciful.

Kaito swallowed his retorts. He decided to speak as little as possible until he returned safely to the castle.

Not receiving an affirmative response, Clueless tilted his head in dissatisfaction.

"You seem displeased... Very well. In order to demonstrate to you the validity of my proposal, allow me to offer you the privilege of observing the heretics under my jurisdiction. Come along."

Clueless went back down the staircase, Kaito in tow. He strode along the dark corridor with vigor in his gait. They met no other clergymen on their journey. As he continued after Clueless, Kaito thought this rather strange. Clueless eventually reached a new staircase and ascended it.

At the top of the stairs was a door with cloth stuffed under it for soundproofing. Clueless turned the knob.

"Look, listen, and learn."

He pushed the door open. The second he did, a bloodcurdling scream rang out.

People were groaning, screaming, writhing, and begging for death. The wide, square inquisition room beyond the door was rank with the thick stench of blood and split down the middle by a set of iron bars.

*   *   *

On the other side of the bars lay a small-scale hellscape.

There were people chained to walls, each completely devoid of hair. Their pasty skin had rivets driven into them. Their bald heads were full of screws, and even as Kaito watched, more were being wound in by people dressed in all white. One woman was tied to an operating table, convulsing as she was slowly sawed apart. An old man pleaded for death, his feet strapped to a white-hot iron plate. A young boy hung from a hook by his tongue, which was also covered in horsehair. The boy wept as he waited for his tongue to dry out completely and tear, dropping him to the floor.

There was also a number of people writhing on the ground. Kaito was unsure how any of them was still alive, and his eyes widened.

He staggered backward a step, but even so, he burned the hellish scene into his eyes. While simultaneously being assailed by terror, he calmly surveilled the scene.

What a merciful proposal the prospect of a painless death now seemed.

Kaito realized how serious Clueless had been.

"I look forward to a favorable response."

Clueless smiled kindly as he pressed the vial of poison into Kaito's hand.

*

The blue rain fell away, and Kaito's vision cleared.

After using the teleportation circle to return to Elisabeth's castle alone, Kaito immediately fell to his knees.

"...Rgh... Blargh..."

He was assaulted by nausea and vertigo. Neither had happened when Elisabeth had been the one activating the circle. Though perhaps his nausea could be attributed to the spectacle he had just been forced to witness, as well as the weight of the choice that had been thrust upon him.

"Shit... That... That was so fucked up..."

After cursing and spitting, he somehow managed to struggle to his feet. He walked through the underground tunnel on unsteady feet.

He remembered the way back. He knew from experience that pain jogged his memory, so a little while back, he'd carved a map of the important bits of the tunnel in his flesh and had Elisabeth heal it for him. She'd been shocked and impressed, and it had hurt like hell, but thanks to that, he was able to avoid getting lost and dying like a fool.

"Dammit... I can't remember—was there something I was supposed to do when I got back?"

Kaito reviewed his remaining duties as he walked. Hina had probably taken care of all the chores for him, and Elisabeth was unlikely to call on him for the rest of the day. She didn't tend to spare much thought for him, so even if she planned on asking him about Clueless, that could be days from now. He had a million things he needed to think about, but for now, all he wanted to do was rest.

If he could just forget about the vial of poison in his breast pocket until the following day, that would be wonderful.

Kaito staggered into the servants' quarters, then made for his room in the corner. He somehow managed to reach the thin door, and its ancient hinges creaked as he opened it.

The instant he did, something soft wrapped around his face.

"Wh-wh-wh-what?"

"Welcome home, Master Kaito! I have awaited your safe return!"

Hina squeezed Kaito tightly. It was only natural for him to be surprised to see her immediately after opening the door.

Hina was on the taller side, so when she leaned over like that, Kaito's face ended up buried right between her breasts. Kaito frantically pulled away, and when he did, Hina's eyes grew wide and sad like a puppy's. The same tactic had gotten him nowhere with Elisabeth, but he was not as immune as she'd been.

Kaito, at a loss for words, averted his gaze from Hina. The cramped room had both a bed and a chair, but neither showed signs of use. Kaito tilted his head to the side, and Hina gave a small hop.

"Lady Elisabeth assured me that you would return, and each moment I waited for you felt like an eternity. I'm deeply sorry that I was unable to accompany you. Oh, I'm so glad you returned unharmed. I was so worried for you that I feared my chest would burst and all my gears would come tumbling out."

"Hold up, Hina... Did you, by any chance, finish the chores and then just stand here all day waiting for me?"

"But of course. Why? Is there a problem?"

"Well, uh... You know, if you really want to wait for me, you can sit down while you wait. It's not like I'm going to get mad at you if you lie down or anything."

Hearing Kaito's words, Hina swayed on her feet. Her cheeks flushed and she pressed down on her mouth.

"Oh my, to receive permission to sleep on my master's precious bed. That is, um, the special privilege of lovers, nay, of husband and wife. In other words, this is a roundabout solicitation—"

"That's not what I meant. Sorry, but I don't have the energy to joke around today..."

Kaito lightly brushed Hina aside and collapsed onto the bed. When he did, he noticed a change. The mattress Elisabeth had given him had been hard, musty, and often damp, but now it was soft and had a pleasant herbal fragrance. Hina had probably carefully washed it, dried it, and scented it for him. But he lacked even the energy to thank her.

His mind a mess, Kaito squeezed his eyes closed. No matter how comfortable it became here, he might soon have to leave the castle. As a traitor. As someone who'd slain his own master. And as compensation for that, he'd get to die painlessly. But no matter how hard he tried, Kaito couldn't imagine himself killing Elisabeth.

When she dies, it'll be of her own accord.

She wasn't the kind of person someone like Kaito could kill. She wasn't the kind of person anyone could kill. But Kaito knew what would become of him if he turned down the proposal. Kaito clutched the vial from over his pocket.

When he did, the bed creaked. A soft, pleasant aroma drew near him. Kaito could tell what it was without having to open his eyes. Hina was lying down beside him. Kaito sighed, then spoke to her again.

"...C'mon, Hina. I really—"

"My apologies, Master Kaito..."

Then she hugged him tight. As she gently cradled his head, her soft hair brushed against his face. Her touch wasn't sexual but sensual: a gesture meant to soothe and comfort. She ran her fingers through his hair. His eyes widened in surprise.

She lay by his side, her twinkling emerald-green eyes rich with adoration. She looked like a woman caring for her troubled husband, and Kaito was at a loss for words in the face of such raw affection.

"…But you seem weary, and this is how lovers comfort their beloved."

Hina gently stroked his hair, running her hands across it again and again. Kaito wondered if this was how children felt when their mothers patted them on the head. Her hands were warm, and their warmth traveled all the way to his heart, transcending reason and language to gently unravel the knots of stress deep inside him.

Surrounded by clean sheets and the warmth of skin, Kaito could feel his eyelids growing heavy.

"…Hina, if you keep doing that…I'm going to fall asleep."

"Isn't that a good thing? You can rest easy. Everything is going to be okay, Master Kaito.

"No matter what happens, I'll protect you."

When she whispered those words into his ear, the knot of stress finally came undone. Kaito realized how unnerved he had been, both by the gruesome display he'd been shown and by the fate that had been thrust upon him. Apparently, he had carried that fear of an agonizing, horrific death all the way back with him.

Oh… I get it now. I was afraid.

He didn't know what would happen now. But here, at least, he

was safe. There was no pain here, and if anyone wished ill on him, Hina said she would protect him.

Back in his old life, no one had ever protected him. This was the first time since he was born that he had ever felt so at ease. He'd never imagined that something so peaceful awaited him after death.

Accompanied by those thoughts, Kaito slowly but surely drifted off to sleep.

He dreamed.
He dreamed, yet he knew it was a dream.

Various images and sensations flashed across his eyes and skin, appearing and disappearing like the light of a revolving lantern.

Enduring countless wounds. Stifling innumerable sorrows. The words *Remember this*, carved into his skin every time he messed up at work. The small, warm tongue that would lick his wounds. The big, round eyes that seemed to suggest they could even love a piece of trash like Kaito. The grief and despair he felt in the moment his windpipe was crushed. Lamenting the fact that he couldn't even scream. The body in the armor. The Knight's eyes. The terrifying spider. Neue's pained smile.

The first kindness he'd received. The words Neue had left him.
The wish Kaito wanted to grant, no matter how impossible it seemed.

The vision of the frail girl, gazing at the outside world. The people, slaughtered without mercy. The wicked, cackling girl.

The distant voice he heard.

"But if she was to form a contract with one of the thirteen demons, her power would grow, and those shackles would be insufficient to restrain her. If that happened, she would become far more dangerous than any of the current contractors."

"You embarrass yourself, Earl."
"You and I—we are fated to die, forsaken by all of creation."

"Having lived the cruel and haughty life of a wolf, I shall die like a lowly sow."
"...For that is the choice I made."

Her long black hair fluttered as she looked over her shoulder. Kaito realized something as he was lost in thought within the dream.

Ah, that's right.
You aren't going to run, are you?

No matter how much pain and despair awaited her, she would take responsibility for her life.

She would take full responsibility for her wretched life.
As the Torture Princess, Elisabeth Le Fanu would bear it.

It was then that Kaito slowly opened his eyes.

Hina held him, still stroking his hair. On her face she wore a peaceful, spellbound smile.

She would have been unable to do anything while stroking his hair. Feeling he'd done something wrong, Kaito quickly got up. Hina seemed reluctant to let him go. She looked at him, then tilted her head to the side.

"Were you able to relax? Compared to earlier, you seem much calmer."

"Yeah, thanks, Hina. Because of you, I was able to get my thoughts in order."

Kaito leaped from the bed and immediately went to leave the room. Sensing his newfound resolve, Hina did not rise to follow him. Kaito stopped in his tracks, then turned around.

Hina sat on the bed, a contented look on her face as she saw him off. Standing in front of the door, Kaito asked her a question.

"Hey, Hina. Would you be sad if I died?"

"In the horrible and unlikely event you were to pass away, Master Kaito, I should surely die as well."

"No, no, no, no, no. What are you talking about?"

"Well, you see, I have absolutely no desire to spend so much as a second in a world where you do not exist."

As if wondering why he would ask such a ridiculous question, Hina looked at him in puzzlement.

Kaito, feeling a headache coming on, pressed down on his forehead. Her response had, once again, been over-the-top. Kaito didn't know what was to become of him. He felt he should tell her not to follow him to the grave, but for the moment he simply returned to bed and stroked her silken silver hair. Hina smiled a warm smile and brought her cheek close to his.

The way she looked at him with unreserved affection, she really did resemble that puppy from so long ago.

Turning her words over in his mind, Kaito muttered as if to confirm his thoughts.

"I see. I guess, if nothing else, I'll have to keep living, then, won't I?"

He made for the hallway. Not long after, he broke off into a run, searching for Elisabeth.

He found her in the throne room. She sat alone in front of the caved-in wall, gazing at the full moon.

Below, the dark forest rustled.

At the place where the beast had been skewered, no traces remained of its corpse. But its bloodstain was etched deep in the earth. Even then, in the dead of night, the ground appeared unsettlingly damp. However, eventually new trees would grow and cover that up as well.

"What happened to that beast's corpse?"

"It burned together with the Knight. But that matters little. Cast your gaze skyward."

Not even turning around as she answered, Elisabeth lifted a gaudy wineglass off the table beside her. She raised it overhead and tilted it from side to side, the full-bodied wine swirling within.

The red wine reflected the white of the moon.

"'Tis a good moon tonight."

She gulped down the moon's reflection, then placed her glass back on the table.

Kaito retrieved the bottle from a silver bowl packed with

spirit-made ice. He poured her another glass of wine, then drew out the vial of poison from his pocket. He poured a drop of the clear liquid into the wine. The beverage briefly changed from a velvety red to a sickening shade of purple before settling back to its original hue.

Kaito handed the glass to Elisabeth, who'd been watching the whole process.

"Very interesting. And what might this be?"

"He told me to poison you."

"Oh-ho, and quite the fine poison it is. Even I might not live after imbibing it. Here, 'tis a special occasion, so I shall give it to you. A glass of wine from your master. Accept it with thanks."

"I respectfully decline. Such a thing would be wasted on me."

"Clueless, eh? And what did he offer you in return? A painless death?"

"I'm surprised you could guess."

"Yes, well. No matter if you live or die, Hell surely awaits you."

Elisabeth spoke bluntly. It seemed she'd more or less suspected what was in store for him. It probably wasn't the case that she'd been hiding it from him; it was more likely that she simply hadn't cared enough to tell him.

She placed the glass back on the table, then gave a large shrug.

"You'd be a fool to take his offer. 'Tis too high a price to pay if death awaits you in the end regardless. But the basic details are half-reasonable. If you were to seek refuge with other members of the Church and avoid being captured by Clueless and his fanatics, the odds that you would be shown mercy and be allowed to keep living are actually quite high."

"Really?"

"You do hail from another world, after all. It would be absurd to accuse you of heresy. True, if you were to survive all thirteen killings, you would likely be treated as one of my possessions, but you still have time remaining. And Hina possesses the knowledge required to link the teleportation circle to the Church. Do as you will."

"Wait... Are you saying that it's all right for me to run away from here?"

"Of course not, fool. You're a puppet of mine. You will remain mine until the moment you break. But unnecessary as it may have been, a servant of mine showed me mercy, and failing to return that mercy would be boorish. Do as you please. But if you intend to flee, you'd best be covert about it. If I catch you deserting, you will face torture."

Yawning, Elisabeth recrossed her legs. She exhaled softly, then reclined against the throne. Her face, cast in profile by the moonlight, had the sharp beauty of a blade.

She said nothing more. Even if Kaito continued waiting, it didn't look like more words would come.

He turned to leave without a sound. But before he could, Elisabeth murmured softly.

"A question, though. Why not just slip me the poison?"

"Hmm?"

"You've despised demons ever since that affair with the Earl. Do you intend to sit idly by and allow the birth of an even more powerful demon? Surely Clueless warned you of the danger."

Elisabeth turned. Her crimson eyes glittered in the moonlight as they fixed on Kaito.

He pondered her question. He hadn't expected it, not from Elisabeth herself. After thinking for a moment, he responded frankly.

"Just like that important-sounding guy from the Church said, I don't think you're the type to make a contract with a demon."

"Oh?"

"You were going to die alone—forsaken by everything in creation, right?"

"Yes, indeed. I shall die with the solitude of a wolf and as pitifully as a sow. All by myself."

"So not even a demon will be by your side, then, right?"

That was Kaito's declaration. She probably wouldn't even have a demon by her side when she died.

Because she'd tortured innocent people and piled up countless corpses, she would be executed.

She herself had chosen that solitary, pitiful death.

Her lips twisted into a smirk. Her shoulders shook, and she burst into pleased laughter. She nodded once, and Kaito left. He exited into the hallway, then cast his gaze up at the clerestory windows and the moonlight they were letting in.

Trying to avoid looking at the creepy images they were casting on the stone floor, he muttered under his breath.

"...Eleven left, huh?"

He clenched his fists, his face full of determination.

The following morning, with Hina's assistance, he fled the castle alone and made for the Church.

✳

Kaito passed through the teleportation circle, which should have been connected to the front gate of the Church's main building. The crimson walls around him finished their work and poured down as showers of blood. But after the crimson cleared, he found himself in a dark room made of packed earth. Kaito's eyes widened. This was the small room that connected to the Church's hidden passages.

He looked around in confusion. When he did, he found the worst possible person waiting for him.

"My, my, did you come seeking the Church's protection?"

Clueless wore a calm smile. Behind him stood a number of his followers, all clad in cylindrical white outfits, their faces covered by hoods.

Surrounded by the men in white, Clueless looked like an executioner leading a body disposal crew.

He peered at Kaito like he was examining a worm, and when he spoke, his tone was full of disappointment.

"My apologies, but it would be inconvenient for me if word got out about the deal I offered you. Since you seem to have declined, I'm afraid we're going to have to settle this in-house. But be at ease. Since you weren't planning on taking my deal, this would have happened sooner or later."

Clueless's followers grabbed Kaito's arms and dragged him roughly to his feet. When they did, a sharp pain suddenly ran through his chest, and he let out a low groan. Clueless gazed at him and raised his voice in exasperation.

"Good grief. It would cause no shortage of problems if you were to continue making noises like that this far up. If you keep doing that, you're liable to wreck your throat. Not that I would mind, of course."

On Clueless's orders, they dragged Kaito away. Based on the direction he was being taken, Kaito discerned that he wasn't going to Clueless's private chamber but to the inquisition room. That was fast. Apparently, Clueless didn't have any more reason to maintain pretenses with him.

Clueless beamed from ear to ear as he reached for the handle to the inquisition room.

"Welcome, dear sinner. Here we will receive you, and here we will deny you."

As he threw it open, the door made a sound like that of the gates of Hell.

They carried Kaito to the other side of the iron bars. As cries of pain surrounded him, he was brought helplessly to the wooden pedestal in the center of the room. They bound his hands and feet in shackles to prevent him from fleeing.

...Looks like I got box-seat tickets.

Kaito cynically mused on his predicament. He hadn't noticed it the last time he was here, but now that he was about to be tortured, he saw a painting of the suffering woman on the ceiling. She wept crimson tears as she gazed down through her veil at the people being tortured. Kaito wondered why she was grieving. He didn't know the specifics of their belief system. But he doubted that the scene she was gazing on was supposed to be a part of it.

Those chosen by God would never wish for such a hellscape. Even Kaito, who was from another world, knew that.

"I mentioned it before, but summoning someone from another

world is quite rare. Through dissection, we should be able to figure out how Elisabeth summoned you. And once we've analyzed
the spell, we'll be able to put the information to great use in
summoning people ourselves. Worry not—your death will not be
in vain. In fact, this should be far preferable to being judged as
Elisabeth's servant. You will be able to serve man and, in doing so,
begin atoning for your sins. Ah, I simply cannot wait."

Clueless looked down at Kaito, barely able to stop himself
from drooling. His eyes were blazing, a far cry from when he'd
been looking at Kaito like a worm a moment ago. He'd acknowl-
edged Kaito's worth, although much of that worth seemed like it
would be present only in the scraps of meat remaining after Kaito
was dissected.

One of the subordinates drew out a large knife. His neighbor
to the right held a pair of bone shears, and the one on the left held
a coping saw. They drew near Kaito, who by this point was well
and truly afraid. He wanted to scream.

His thoughts burning, he opened his mouth.

"When you say 'we,' do you mean you and the demon you
contracted with?"

Clueless's smile froze on his face. Kaito felt the familiar sensation of the pieces clicking into place. Clueless was the kind of
person who was weak to surprise attacks. In Kaito's past life, one
of the people his father had blackmailed was a company president
who had been cooking his books, and the president had often
worn that exact same expression. Kaito heaved a heavy sigh before
continuing on.

"The thing is, I was connected to the Church's front gate, but my intention all along was to come looking for you. Your interference saved me some time. I wanted to run, but I couldn't... After seeing this hell, I couldn't just leave things like this."

Kaito could move his head a little, and he peered through the iron bars. Even now, a hellscape was unfolding around him. Right next to his pedestal was a man with his chest torn open and his stomach exposed, writhing in agony. There was a mother and her child, bound by thick strings and both coughing up foamy blood.

Kaito didn't have a particularly strong sense of justice. Normally, self-sacrifice would be the last thing on his mind. But even he had his limits. He couldn't just let this nauseating spectacle continue.

"When I saw this hell, I realized just how suspicious you seemed. Demons get their power from people's pain, from the discord in their souls that pain causes. And when I saw the torture you were performing in the name of inquisition, I got the same impression I get from demons... After all, it didn't exactly look like you were just torturing people to get them to confess to their heresy."

The people around him were on the verge of death, writhing in unending agony.

The worst things one could imagine were being done to these heretics. This kind of torture could only be the work of demons.

"How could they stay alive with their bodies full of rivets, with their bodies diced to pieces, with their stomachs torn open? Maybe if you were taking serious measures to keep them alive, the facade would be more convincing, but most of them were just left to suffer. When you first showed me this room, I unconsciously burned the image into my mind, so when I thought about it later on, I was sure of it. Their lives were being forcibly extended by a demon's power… Which means that this little party definitely isn't Church approved."

When they'd gone through Clueless's secret underground passageway, they hadn't run across any other members of the Church.

If this torture was official Church business, and similar things were going on elsewhere, then there should have been more people coming and going, people doing things like transporting heretics and cleaning up blood. But no one had been in those passages but Clueless and his men. Kaito hadn't seen a single other person from the Church.

Clueless had kept Kaito from meeting any of the other clergymen, obstinately concealing them from him.

In other words, his actions were in defiance of the Church.

"I also found it interesting that you resolved to kill Elisabeth all on your own. When the Church came to her for help, I have to imagine they didn't have anywhere else to turn. They were probably at their wits' ends. Imagine. Hiring a sow to deal with the pigs. Yet, in spite of this, a supposed member of the Church came to the castle in secret and tried to get me to kill her. The prevention of the birth of an almighty demon—it sounds like a reasonable excuse at first, but after you got rid of her, how did you plan on dealing with the remaining demons? There could only be one reason you wanted to get rid of your prize hound after she'd only killed two of the thirteen demons—you're one of the thirteen."

Given that there had been a contractor among the Royal Knights, it didn't seem strange for there to be one in the Church as well. And having been tasked with disposing of heretics, he'd found himself in a convenient position to accumulate pain. He'd even tried to use his position to eliminate a potent foe. But he'd done it too hastily and far too sloppily.

That was what happened when one failed to keep up appearances while looking down on others.

Clueless had treated him like a worm, and Kaito laughed scornfully as he looked up at his face.

"I'm right, aren't I, Clueless? Well, the only reason I was able to notice was because Hina helped me get my thoughts in order, but still."

"Is that all you have to say, you doddering little doll?"

Clueless smiled calmly, neither confirming nor denying Kaito's accusations. But Kaito didn't fail to notice the vein slightly bulging on his forehead.

If he hadn't been bound, Kaito would have shrugged, but he settled for a nod.

"Yup, that's all for me. I found the demon. I set the snare. Now it's the Torture Princess's turn."

"Oh, but the teleportation circle is closed off from this side. You imbecile! You have no cards left to play!"

Clueless laughed. Kaito's eyes grew cold as he wondered if Clueless was an idiot. Kaito had watched Clueless meddle with the teleportation circle before. It was obvious that Kaito had seen this coming.

Kaito took a deep breath, then exhaled sharply.

And his stomach hurt.

"It only seats one, but I've got a circle right here."

A puzzled look spread across Clueless's face, but in the next moment, his eyes opened wide. He tore off Kaito's shirt.

Several leather belts were wrapped around Kaito's midsection.

A crimson teleportation circle glowed beneath the high-quality hide. Clueless frantically removed the belts with his bone shears, then tore off the dressing beneath them. When he saw where the teleportation circle's light was coming from, he gasped.

"...You son of a bitch."

"It's real handy, how much blood this body can lose without dying."

The teleportation circle was carved on Kaito's stomach. The cuts were deep, and blood gushed out of them. Even so much as breathing sent sharp pains rippling through his chest. When Clueless's men had been dragging him a moment ago, he had thought he might die from the pain. But the time he spent gritting his teeth was paying off.

"As my servant, even you could use your blood to summon something to your side."

Elisabeth had mentioned that once, some time ago. Clueless clutched the shears and tried to add fresh cuts to Kaito's wounds. But he was too late, and the teleportation circle began violently glowing. Crimson flower petals flew through the air, and darkness began to spread. Clueless's eyes widened, and he shouted as he drew back.

"Stay away... Stay away, Elisabeeeeeeeeeeeeeeeeeeeeeeeeeeeee eth!"

"Ah, but how could I, after hearing my name called so passionately?"

A voice rife with mockery rang out, and the darkness surged forth. Crimson flower petals fluttered throughout the prison. The petals then turned to raindrops, showering the room in red.

Elisabeth, drenched in blood, made her appearance from the teleportation circle. Her elegant black hair and draping dress wafted gently, and her ample bosom bounced. She landed on her heels, right on Kaito's gaping wound.

Her smile was sinister, and ignoring Kaito's screams of pain, she snapped her fingers.

"Nothing fancy for the small fry, I think. *Death by Hanging.*"

Straw ropes dropped from the ceiling and wrapped themselves around the necks of Clueless's men. It was almost comical how quickly they got yanked into the air. Their necks made loud popping sounds as their spines snapped, their respiratory tracts collapsed, and their veins burst. The hoods that had been concealing their faces plopped off.

Their faces were made of huge, festering sarcomas. They weren't humans. They were underlings.

Their corpses dangled from the ceiling.

"This can't... Damn you. Damn you!"

Clueless's hands shook as he grabbed the necklace from his collar. He tried to mutter something. But when he did, steel shackles bound around his wrists. His gaze froze on Elisabeth and her smile.

"It seems you're fond of pain, hmm?"

"Aaaaaaaaaaaaaaaaaaaaaaaaaaaaaaaaaaaargh!"

The shackles jerked, and his wrists snapped. Fragments of bone pierced his skin from within. He screamed, writhing in agony. But suddenly, his arms slid out of the fetters binding them.

His whole body was soon covered in venom. His thick blond hair fell out in clumps, and his cassock burst off. As his limbs continued to swell, he leaped into the air. Now resembling a fleshy meat-frog, he pushed his flesh through the prison's iron bars and fled for the corridor.

For some reason, Elisabeth's face contorted in surprise after seeing Clueless's massive, hideous form.

"That man... He possesses an unnatural amount of magical power, but he is no demon! He's a weakling, a mere underling!"

"Really? That's good news, right? That means you can take him out easily."

"Of course it isn't good, you fool! He's a member of the Church! Surely you jest... The only demon a member of the Church would encounter is..."

Elisabeth snapped her fingers. The restraints on Kaito's arms and legs popped open. Crimson petals collected around his wound and forcibly infused it with Elisabeth's blood. The petals also wrapped a fresh leather belt around him. Kaito screamed at the sudden pain of the forcible transfusion and hemostasis.

"Gah! What're you doing? Dammit, Elisabeth, that hurts!"

"Follow me if you wish. Or stay, but I may return late, or take another route back to the castle altogether. It would be on you to stay alive until you received proper treatment."

"*Not* following you doesn't seem like much of a choice, then, does it?!"

After struggling to his feet, Kaito took off after Elisabeth. He'd only recovered a little from his blood loss. If he could ignore the pain, he'd probably be able to keep up with her.

Having cleared the door, the meat-frog was clumsily running through the passage. Elisabeth waved her hand at it. Darkness and crimson petals coalesced, then became a massive spiked wheel.

The wheel spun toward it, but it vanished midpath as if repelled by something.

For a second, Kaito thought he saw a black dog's tail sticking out of the frog's back.

The meat-frog turned and then, with a relieved expression, took off again, even faster than before.

"That reaction... Could it really be him?!"

Elisabeth's voice was tinged with uncharacteristic desperation. Even though her foe was a mere underling, she unsheathed the Executioner's Sword of Frankenthal.

The meat-frog hopped up a larger set of stairs, then smashed through the door at the top. Upon seeing the frog, an old, gentle-looking clergyman carrying a bundle of scrolls screamed and fell on his rear. A group of believers hid behind a young clergyman who'd apparently been leading them around. Kaito hadn't expected the Church to be such an ordinary, upright organization.

The path the meat-frog was taking led it into an orderly, neat marble room. It continued to flee, spraying foamy venom as it went. As it made for the worship hall, Elisabeth swung her sword in its direction.

"*Gibbet!*"

The darkness spiraled in a long, vertical pattern, and a cage barely wide enough to fit a person standing up straight clamped around the meat-frog, wringing massive amounts of venom from it. Chains surrounded the cage. Even if the meat-frog broke out of the cage, the chains would still restrain it. But the next moment, Elisabeth's body quivered and she dropped to her knees.

"Rrrgh... Mm... Ah, my body..."

The cage crumbled, returning to darkness and petals. The

chains, too, lost their power, collapsing to the floor and wriggling a few times before vanishing.

"Elisabeth!"

Patterns of scarlet characters snaked across her body. Kaito's golem features tried to decipher their meaning but failed. His knowledge bank told him it was the Word of God, unable to be translated or vocalized.

The scripture was etched all over her body like burns. She looked as though she had been branded.

So those were the shackles the Church had put on her. But why did they activate just now?

"It burns... Rrrgh... Wh-why...? Who...?"

Even though she was down on her hands and knees, Elisabeth shot a hate-filled glare to her side. Up on the altar was a clergyman, clutching his necklace and waving it side to side as he chanted a prayer. With every verse, the patterns on Elisabeth's skin flared scarlet. She screamed in bloodcurdling rage.

"Not *me*, you imbecile! That's the one you should be stopping! Fool!"

The meat-frog mowed down worshippers and smashed through pews as it headed deeper into the church.

A band of guards had finally assembled, but the meat-frog mercilessly routed them. Pressed beneath its massive belly, their bones shattered in their armor. But even in his confusion, the clergyman never stopped his prayer.

Kaito dashed up the short steps, then forcefully stuck out his hand.

"What—?"

"I'm borrowing this, old man!"

Kaito snatched the necklace off the man's wrinkly neck and threw it. Elisabeth stood, then took off like a newly fired arrow. But she was still covered in serious burn marks.

Elisabeth ran, continuing to be tormented by the scripture, and Kaito followed after her.

The hallway was littered with the guards' battered corpses, and they only grew more prevalent the farther the two of them got. They seemed to have been guarding an imposing door, but that door was now wide open.

An impressive office lay behind it. An old man wearing a diadem and a gold vestment sat dead atop a velvet chair, his body crushed from the waist down.

The wall behind the man had been smashed to pieces.

Beyond the wall was a hidden passage, covered on all surfaces by the faint glow of the Word of God. With every step the meat-frog took down it, its body frothed violently as its flesh burned. But Elisabeth was no different. The instant she'd dashed into the corridor, the patterns on her body flared up again, and she let out a scream of agony.

"Rrrgh… Aaaaaargh! Ah, ah!"

"Elisabeth, don't be stupid!"

Hurriedly, Kaito rushed to support Elisabeth. As he propped her up, he endured the pain in his stomach and walked forward. The meat-frog, somehow still alive, reached the end of the passageway. It clung to the wall and pleaded, shedding a flood of tears all the while.

"Oh my Lord. I was mistaken. Hungry for power, I left you sealed away. Had I but believed in you, I never would have done such a thing. But now I offer you my everything. I will free you as a sign of my devotion. So please, save me from that demonic woman."

The meat-frog vomited something out. From within the mass of phlegm, it retrieved a golden key.

After intricately tracing the Words of God and offering up words of prayer, it inserted the key into what appeared to be a featureless wall. A clicking noise rang out, and the wall flashed violently before vanishing.

Deep darkness and a sharp chill flowed out from inside. In the center of the persistent darkness sat an Iron Chair.

Upon it sat a black-haired man.

The man slowly looked up. His dark, tangled hair rustled, and his crimson eyes glittered. From what Kaito could see of his facial features behind the hair, he possessed a certain androgynous beauty. But the instant he looked at the man, his throat swelled up, intimidated, and he understood something.

That man was terrifying. Even though he possessed a beautiful human form, he was no human. He was something repulsive.

Yet, despite all that, his face looked somehow familiar.

Without a sound, the belts holding the man's arms and legs burned to ash. He slowly stood, as though he was rising from a throne. Clad in prison garb, he plucked a needle free from his back, and blood gushed out. Yet, his expression did not change in the slightest.

His eyes were vacant, as if he were in a waking dream.

Clueless, the meat-frog, crawled toward the man and knelt

awkwardly before him with eyes that screamed for mercy. With-out even looking at the meat-frog, the man raised a foot.

He then brought his bare foot down on its head. The frog's massive eyes popped right out at the impact.

"Ble—"

Dark-red blood began spilling forth. The meat-frog's head had been abruptly crushed, and its gray brain tissue oozed out. But even surrounded by blood, the man was still emotionless. He looked back up, as if he'd simply stepped on an ordinary frog that had jumped in his path.

It was then that he saw Elisabeth, standing in the entrance, for the first time.

His absentminded expression vanished, replaced by an impos-sibly charming smile.

"Elisabeth."

His voice, filled with fervent adoration, was the same as the one Kaito had heard in the castle's Treasury.

"VLAAAAAAAAAAAAAAAAAAAAAAAD!"

Elisabeth howled, shoving Kaito away. He flew into the wall and crumpled without a word.

She rushed into the room, waving the Executioner's Sword of Frankenthal. She slashed at the empty air, and hundreds of chains bore down on the man like a torrent. But the scripture still burned in her flesh, and her chains lacked their usual strength. Even so, they would have been sufficient to shred the Knight they had

fought before to pieces, but a canine black tail whipped through the air and blocked every last one.

Grrrrrrrrr, grrrrrrrrrrrr, grrrrrrrrrrrr.

Out of nowhere, an enormous black dog squatted by the man's side. It was a first-class hound, with lustrous fur and rippling muscles.

The black dog had the stench of a beast, and its mouth and eyes burned with hellfire. While it didn't look hideous in the slightest, every instinct Kaito had screamed out to him that it was more dangerous than any demon they had faced yet. But for whatever reason, he didn't feel an ounce of fear. His mind was unusually numb.

Face-to-face with the embodiment of death, his sense of fear had been completely paralyzed.

This thing was in an overwhelmingly different realm than the ugly, twisted demons.

The black dog stuck out its head. With movement so efficient you could almost call it beautiful, it leaped toward Elisabeth with its sharp fangs. But right before it could clamp down on her slender frame, the man shook his head. The dog stopped, and with a dreamlike gaze, the man vanished.

When he did, so did the suffocating pressure that had filled the room. Kaito had seen everything from the passageway. After finally reaching the room, he looked around in a stupor.

"Wait… Where did he go? Or rather, more importantly, who *was* that?"

"The Kaiser."

"What?"

Elisabeth answered his question in a stiff voice. He tilted his head to the side.

Seeing Kaito's poor grasp of the situation, she repeated herself.

"The Kaiser has returned to his homeland."

5

The Birthplace of the Torture Princess

Elisabeth sat in her usual room, one leg over the other.

Atop the ball-and-claw throne, she stared into the gloomy, overcast sky. An orb of pale-blue light hovered in front of her. Kaito hadn't been told the specifics, but as the orb slowly rotated, it projected the image of someone who seemed rather important. However, despite appearing on the front of the orb no matter which way you looked at it, his face was so blurry, it looked like it was encased in a cloud of fog. It was difficult to pick out a single distinct feature.

The mysterious figure spoke in a low voice, cold as ice.

"We had been discussing transferring the Kaiser to the capital, so his seal was incomplete. Furthermore, Clueless had a talent for currying favor, and as such was able to glean the strictly confidential location where the Kaiser was imprisoned, as well as the method to free him, from the officer in charge of the Kaiser's detainment. Furthermore, much of the Church's leadership, myself included, were heading for the capital to prepare for the festival, leaving the Church's defenses lacking... This incident was brought about by various deficiencies and misfortunes on our part."

"Just come out and say it was preventable, you fool. Enough with the public relations—get on with the more pertinent matters."

"The Church formally demands that you, Elisabeth Le Fanu, kill or apprehend the Kaiser."

Elisabeth sighed a silent victory at the orb's declaration. She recrossed her legs and grinned.

"So it falls to me to clean up your mess yet again. And so it has been, time and time again. Once more does your God sit idle, leaving you to fend for yourselves. All you have to protect you is the authority you wield. You leash dogs in the name of your god, then sit back and crack your whips at them."

"We lack the power to contest with those monsters. That is why we are forced to rely on you. But that is in no way contradictory to the fact that God is constantly by our side. He tests us, true, but His blessings are with us as they are for all His children."

"Ha! Such fine platitudes you regurgitate, swindler! According to your doctrine, are those men, reduced to grotesque forms by their demonic contracts, not also *His* creations? Am I, Torture Princess that I am, not a creature of your God? Where are His blessings for us, may I ask? Your words are rife with hypocrisy!"

"His blessings have always been with you. God is eternally merciful. If only you would realize that, even now, He is surely shedding tears of blood even as He punishes you, hoping that you may atone for your sins. I have known you since you were a child, Elisabeth, daughter of my dear friend...and you have every reason to hate demons."

Elisabeth's eyebrow twitched. Her expression darkened, and she drew her lips together. From her side, Kaito viewed her expression with caution. But as she turned to glare at him, he quickly straightened his posture.

Paying no heed to Elisabeth's silence, the voice continued.

"Take care not to forget the words we inscribed on your sword. 'You are free to act as you will. But pray that God shall be your salvation. For the beginning, the middle, and the end all lie in the palm of His hand.' *The Church placed a number of restraints on the Kaiser, as well. We put them all in motion earlier today. They will last seven days, so that is how long you have to hand down his punishment."*

His tone didn't change as he notified her of her time limit. It carried none of the weight of a threat. That fact was precisely what drove fear deep into Kaito's heart. Standing beside Elisabeth, his mind spun.

Seven days, huh? Will she even be able to do anything about the Kaiser in that little time? And what'll happen if she can't?

What kinds of calamities would befall the world in that event? With nothing left to say, the voice concluded with a final, chilling order.

"Before the day of your death, try to do some good at least."

The light in the orb faded, and it fell to the ground with a delicate *plop*. Kaito reached down and picked it up. The orb had been made of thin paper. He had no idea where the light had been coming from.

Still confused, he looked up at Elisabeth and asked:

"So what was that about?"

"Communications from Godot Deus, the head of the Church. Ever the gaudy antique, that one is."

She shook her head, not saying any more. As she stared off into space, Kaito decided to start by asking her the question that weighed heaviest on his mind.

"So do you have any idea where the Kaiser went?"

"Indeed."

Her answer was immediate. At once, Kaito was filled with relief. The difficulty of their task varied immensely depending on whether or not they could pinpoint the Kaiser's location.

Elisabeth squinted as she gazed through a hole in the collapsed wall, as if she was looking at something far off in the distance. Before her extended a seemingly infinite expanse of dark trees and faintly glimmering gray clouds.

★   ★   ★

"The Kaiser has returned home. To my castle, the place of my birth."

Why had the Kaiser returned to Elisabeth's birthplace?

Why had the Kaiser called out her name so affectionately?

Kaito waited for her to elaborate. But Elisabeth said nothing more, and Kaito didn't ask. They simply stood, gazing through the hole in the wall.

Their silence persisted. Wind blew in from outside, carrying with it the scent of rain. Elisabeth finally breathed in deeply and then exhaled. She clicked her tongue, then stood with enough force to knock over her chair.

"...Let's go."

"...Mm-hmm."

Her voice bristled with ire, and Kaito nodded.

The next moment, he felt a sharp kick to his leg. Apparently, his response had been unbecoming of a servant.

✳

Elisabeth's hometown lay beyond a high wall.

Out of all the territory the noble Le Fanu house had once possessed, this castle town was special. This was where the Torture Princess's bloodstained legend had begun.

The town was arranged like a fan, with the splendid white-walled Le Fanu castle at its center and a steep mountain range forming its backdrop. And it made good use of its unique topography. The wall surrounding it formed a summoning platform for mythical beasts and provided a layer of defense for emergencies. But now, that wall served a different purpose.

With its gate shut firmly, the wall sealed off the city. If one was to take even a single step beyond that threshold, they would find themselves surrounded by death.

That towering barrier now served as a massive gravestone for the town.

According to rumor, the Torture Princess herself, Elisabeth Le Fanu, had once sealed that gate, summoned torture devices all around the town, and set them on every last resident. The banquet of slaughter lasted three days and nights, and during that period, ceaseless screams of anguish filled the air like a grand symphony.

She'd used the slaughter in this town as an opportunity to surpass the Plain of Skewers and the Dance Macabre in the Village by the Mountains to birth more corpses than ever before.

…The more I learn, the worse it gets.

All of this was information Kaito had learned from Elisabeth herself.

When he'd asked her about the place they were heading, Elisabeth had tossed him a document the Church had assembled, titled *Records of the Torture Princess*. Seeing his appalled face after reading the opening anecdote, she gave a "Humph."

★   ★   ★

"Just who exactly did you think I was? I am Elisabeth Le Fanu, the Torture Princess.

"I may be hunting demons, but I am still the grandest criminal this world possesses, one who not even death can redeem."

The land where Elisabeth, Kaito, and Hina currently stood was the place from which all those morbid tales originated.

A charred ruin extended before them.

After the slaughter, those in charge of disposing of the massive quantity of corpses had been at a loss as to what to do, and they eventually settled on simply lighting everything past the walls ablaze. The fire had been left to burn for seven days and seven nights. After the inferno was extinguished, however, no attempt was made to retrieve the bodies. The town was simply marked as "cursed" and blockaded.

Kaito, upon seeing the mounds of human bones peeking out among the cracks of the carbonized rubble, murmured softly.

"Well, that's not a pretty sight."

"Nay, not in the slightest. The Church wrote it off as having been 'abandoned by God.'"

Elisabeth spoke as if it had nothing to do with her, and Kaito gave a curt nod.

There was no exaggeration to that wording. The rotting houses, the torture devices, and the innumerable skeletons strewn about the rubble invoked images of religious paintings of Hell. The brick foundations of houses with their roofs burned off formed the background, and the countless skeletons skewered on iron stakes practically looked like offerings to Diablo.

*   *   *

In contrast with the morbid scene, the white castle stood tall and radiant. It alone was unmarred by soot or degradation.

It looked almost like a toy, placed atop a pile of mud and ash.

Elisabeth, the person responsible for the horrid state of this bizarre landscape, briefly clicked her tongue.

"Tch. I'm hardly in a position to complain, but the air here is unpleasant. Take care not to let your guard down. The Kaiser has already settled in. Even I haven't the faintest idea of what awaits us, but whatever it may be, you can be sure that it won't be pleasant."

"Yes, ma'am. I will stay battle-ready. Master Kaito, I beseech you to stay behind me so that you may avoid harm."

"Ah, right. Thanks."

Kaito nodded, then obediently moved to Hina's rear. Hina grinned as she gave a bow.

"Be at ease. No matter the cost, I shall protect you, Master."

Her words dripped with their usual admiration, but in her arms, she brandished a massive halberd.

The weapon cast a fiendish silhouette, and it was much taller than she was. Its lance head was disturbingly thick, and a fat, curved sword was attached to the ax head. It must have been tremendously heavy, but Hina carried it with the same grace and dignity she would carry a teapot to a tea party.

Kaito couldn't tell if the scene before him was a joke or a nightmare. He felt light-headed from the vertigo the spectacle inspired within him.

Elisabeth had been right—the air here was unpleasant. The atmosphere, too, carried an uncomfortable heat. It almost felt as though that fire was still smoldering somewhere deep in the earth. All the bodies should have rotted away or turned to ash by now, but Kaito occasionally caught a strong whiff of something rotting. He couldn't help but feel that the sentiments and regrets of those who had died here were decomposing like their flesh, accumulating into a thick muck.

And the hatred and malice that muck was spewing forth were directed at a single woman.

Loathsome Elisabeth, repulsive Elisabeth, cruel, hideous Elisabeth!

A curse upon you, a curse upon you, a curse, a curse, an eternal curse upon you, Elisabeth!

The entire town joined together in a voiceless roar. It was no mere trick of the ear.

After all, this was a place of death. It was Elisabeth's hometown, the place where the Torture Princess was born. But the woman in question ignored the pressure bearing down on her from all sides. Elisabeth walked on with a ruler's composure.

What's going through your head right now?

Kaito couldn't begin to imagine how she felt. But he had no idea of what to ask or how to ask her. He wasn't even sure if there was any reason to ask in the first place. Besides, figuring out how to deal with the Kaiser took top priority.

He simply followed after Elisabeth, walking across roads of hardened muck and ash.

The town was littered with mementos of the atrocities that took place there. Half-buried skulls were lined up in rows like a vegetable plot. A large tree had survived the fire, and dangling from its branches were three human skeletons and one dog skeleton bound by wire. No doubt it had been set up so that when the canine struggled to get free, its claws would dig into the survivors.

Kaito knit his brows at the appalling scene. Suddenly, one skull slowly looked up from its pile.

"...Huh?"

"Hmm? What is it, Kaito?"

"Look over there."

A skeleton was leisurely tilting its neck, its hollow eye sockets trained directly on Elisabeth. Kaito rubbed his eyes. But no matter how many times he checked, the pile of bones that should have been lying prone was staring straight at them. That was when it happened.

Click, click, clack.

A band of skeletons appeared from behind a dilapidated house, making miserable, dry clacking noises as they leaped onto the main road. Spears had been thrust all the way up their rear ends and protruded from their mouths, and their spines were riddled with splinters. Their arms and legs were trimmed off. With their tragic bodies, they danced in the street, spinning with what appeared to be joy.

Seeing how the heinous torture had warped their bones, Kaito gasped. Noticing his pause, one of the skeletons drew near him. As if entreating him, it extended what remained of its hand, and Kaito grabbed it without thinking. When he did, it yanked its inverted wrist hard. But then, with a clattering sound, it shattered.

"Don't you dare lay a hand on Master Kaito, you lackey!"

"Ah, whoops."

Kaito hurriedly hid behind Hina again. The skeletons rushed

at them, one after another. But their main target, Elisabeth, didn't even spare them a glance.

"Heavens, how noisy they are."

She yawned, then clicked her heels as she continued walking. Each time she did, iron stakes burst forth from the ground in a shower of darkness and crimson petals. But even when they were sown to the ground, the skeletons merely collapsed into piles of bones, then re-formed out of the undamaged ones to resume their chase. Even with Hina swinging her halberd and Elisabeth driving them away, the corpses seemed unkillable.

Kaito could feel his chest freeze as he realized that these were all people Elisabeth had killed.

As if joining a parade, a fresh batch of skeletons rushed them. Finally, Elisabeth clicked her tongue.

"Just how long do you intend to keep up these petty, petty, petty little attacks? Come now. Surely you've realized that even if a century passed, these skeletons would never be able to so much as scratch me, haven't you? Why not just show yourself? You don't mean to tell me you have no more cards to play, do you? How pathetic that would be."

The three of them traveled east, repelling skeletons all the while. They arrived at the main road leading to the castle.

The road was wide and neatly paved with brick, as if in consideration of carriage traffic. It was lined with melted metal signs, frames of once-splendid houses, and ash-covered shops with their shingled roofs intact. Even in its current state of disrepair, the main road still contained traces of the town's lost prosperity. But at the moment, standing in the doorway to this place's tragic past was an ominous figure.

★   ★   ★

There was a tall woman, wearing a mourning dress as if she was grieving for the countless dead.

Her face was hidden behind black lace, and her lustrous black hair cascaded down her back as she hung her head. Everything she was wearing, from her silk gloves and her long skirt to the standing collar covering her neck, was black. She was oddly thin, and her conservative dress left much to the imagination. The only place she wasn't small was her chest, which was oddly alluring. Her wide-brimmed hat was decorated with a fragrant collection of white lilies.

The flowers were somber, like the kind one would leave at a grave, and their elegant glimmer was the only deviance from her otherwise all-black outfit.

Elisabeth stopped, then posed an irritated question to the woman.

"Suspicious woman in black, are you the necromancer responsible for these bothersome attacks?"

"…So you do not hesitate, even when faced with the victims you tormented, those you defiled, and those you killed without mercy?"

Her voice was deep for a woman's, yet it reverberated somewhat softly in the ear. Elisabeth furrowed her brow. She narrowed her crimson eyes, as if searching her memory for something.

Kaito, standing behind her, tilted his head as well. He wasn't used to her showing her enemies an emotion other than anger or frustration. The woman continued in a voice like clear water.

"Are you perhaps saying that after you've finished your meat, you care not what happens to the bones?"

"Indeed, that is what I was about to say... Wait... That voice, that manner of speaking... You can't be...?"

The woman offered no response to Elisabeth's mutterings. She instead picked up the hem of her long skirt from the piles of ash on the ground, then lifted it high enough that her thighs were visible. It didn't look like she was wearing panties, which made the amount of skin she was revealing even more precarious. Bones tumbled out of her skirt, grazing her skin as they fell.

The bones rattled as they resumed their original forms. The woman stroked the skull of one of the newly formed skeletons as if it were a cat. Looking at the fully formed skeletons, Kaito found himself at a loss for words.

Their hands and feet were twisted, and their backs were stretched out into a bridge formation. They scuttled about on all fours. When they were alive, their bodies had likely been fixed in place so long that they could no longer walk normally.

And the tiny skeletons had all belonged to children.

The skeletons clattered as they scuttled along the ground toward Elisabeth. They let out noises from the gaps between their teeth, almost like they were trying to scream. But without a shred of hesitation or mercy, Elisabeth swung her leg sideways.

"Enough!"

She crushed the children's skulls under the heel of her foot. Their bones scattered. Her kick sent a gust of wind at the woman, and her hat blew clean off and fell to the ground. The woman's face, no longer concealed by black lace, came into view.

She smiled. She was beautiful, but her plush lips, almond-shaped eyes, and the mole on her cheek gave her a plain impression.

"You haven't kept in touch, Madam Elisabeth."

Her ashen-blue eyes welled up with tears as she bowed deeply. After picking up her hat and brushing off the dirt, she raised her head and replaced the hat diagonally such that it no longer covered her face. As she spoke, she narrowed her eyes in nostalgia.

"I see you haven't changed a bit, young miss. Even though I suggested time and time again that it might be for the best if you did something about that temper of yours."

"So... You are Marianne, then?"

For the first time, Elisabeth's voice shook. The woman nodded happily. After seeing Elisabeth's rare reaction, Kaito instinctively asked:

"Marianne?"

"She was once my tutor. Now, what are you doing here? As I recall, you were an ordinary woman, one with a decent education and passable looks, but one who was irritatingly fastidious and who missed her chance to marry. So why are you here, and why are you a necromancer?"

"Is that a serious question, young miss? Do you seriously believe that I could have kept on being an ordinary woman after seeing that brutal spectacle?"

The woman, Marianne, answered in a singsong voice. Her thin hands, clad in black silk gloves, began to move.

Each time she brought her hands up and down, the skeletons scattered about the street hopped in sync with them as though threads were manipulating them. Marianne continued talking as she directed their silly little dance.

"Oh, by all rights, I should have simply fled after being over-looked by the infamous Torture Princess. I should have fled the town, moved to the countryside, and lived out the rest of my days in silence. But I couldn't. Not after seeing my own pupil, adorably willful yet fundamentally meek as she was, gleefully summoning torture devices and slaughtering the innocent. After seeing the hell you created, young miss, I thought to myself..."

Marianne peered up. The look she directed at Elisabeth was one of remorse and pity.

"...This ordeal was my fault, born from my own shortcomings. Had I only been a better tutor... Had I only been able to guide you down a proper path, then even when your parents died, you would not have strayed so far. The responsibility fell on my shoulders. I failed to save you, young miss."

"You speak drivel. What part of this was your fault? You think too highly of yourself, Marianne. Cruelty has been my nature since childhood, and your teachings did naught to sway that for better or worse. Anything you could have done would have been akin to dust in the wind. It would have held no meaning and left no traces."

Elisabeth raised one black fingernail. Kaito, anticipating a torture device to appear, gulped. But Elisabeth didn't summon anything. She simply pointed off in the distance.

"Leave. I know not why you appeared before me after all this time, but I don't care to see your face again. You did much for me in my childhood, in the days I could not venture outside. I shall overlook our meeting today. But I shan't grant you a third chance. Vanish from my sight. Leave now, and you may yet die a peaceful death."

After being attacked, Elisabeth is going to let this woman go?

Kaito's jaw was on the ground. He thought back to the image of Elisabeth's youth he'd seen. He tried imagining this fussy yet kind woman by that frail girl's side.

He could envision that scene, of a tutor and her willful pupil side by side, surprisingly easily.

The fact that such a scene had once played out in reality was likely the source of Elisabeth's mercy. But Marianne didn't seem likely to take Elisabeth up on her offer.

Marianne clutched at her sides, hugging herself so tightly, you could make out the bones in her fingers.

"It's my fault... It's my fault you turned out so twisted... I have to—"

"Get ahold of yourself, Marianne! Listen when other people are—"

"Oh, young miss!"

The bones in Marianne's fingers began to creak. The skeletons at her feet began hopping up and down as if in response to her violent passion. They then collapsed, abandoning their human forms, and all combined together into a massive tower. The tower collapsed onto Elisabeth, creaking as it fell.

Elisabeth shrugged. But the next moment, an explosion rocked the bones and they were sent flying from within.

A pale horse leaped free from the tower.

"Wh—?!"

Elisabeth's eyes widened. Kaito, too, was at a loss for words. The Knight was supposed to be dead, yet there sat a Knight astride the photoluminescent horse with great pomp and circumstance. Then again, this wasn't *truly* the Knight.

The Knight standing before them was made of rotting flesh. His horse's chest was dissolved to expose ribs. As for the Knight, maggots and manure seeped from the gaps in his helmet. Even for someone who'd been resurrected, his body was in poor shape. But just like the original, the horse's hoof steps were accompanied by bolts of lightning.

As he spurred his steed forward, the rider pulled his lance of lightning from thin air.

"Bone Mill!"

Elisabeth swung a flat, spiked hammer. It smashed into the Knight's rotting flesh, crushed his bones, and scattered his body to the wind. But right before his destruction, the Knight smashed his lance against the ground. His decaying body had been weak, but the power of his attacks was nothing to laugh at.

Marianne, who had been casting her gaze downward, looked up with a smile of utter devotion.

"It's things like that that make me love you so, young miss!"

She shouted in ecstasy, her cheeks reddening. Her breath was heavy, as though she was trying to contain her excitement, and she squeezed on her supple breasts as she hugged herself.

Elisabeth took a step back, her face visibly stiffening. Kaito, equally uncomfortable, felt a bead of cold sweat drip down his back. Marianne stood in front of them, her eyes burning.

She was clearly not in her right mind.

Marianne muttered gleefully, clutching her chest even tighter.

"The sins you bear are beyond your ability to atone for, young miss. You will die unappreciated, unloved, cursed, and despised. I am the only one who can save you. I am the only one who would dare to try. But that is my duty, the one assigned to me the moment I failed to stop you. My mind is made up, young miss."

Marianne licked her thick lips. Drool dribbled all the way down to her chin.

"I will kill you with my own two hands!"

"The Knight, eh...? You've picked up a rather strange talent. While I fail to understand his intention, *that man* doubtlessly instigated this. Just how much power did the Kaiser confer upon you?"

Elisabeth had ignored her passionate confession, and Marianne simply smiled in response to the question Elisabeth posed.

With a sound like a percussion instrument, the bones assembled themselves into a tower once more. A bonfire-like blue flame swirled up inside it. The scene resembled a bizarre ritual, and a new, grotesque Knight fell from the flames. The tower rose again and again, each time producing a copy of the Knight.

In front of them, the tower created a row of smaller boxes. Out of each box leaped a meat-frog. Their countless soggy hands and feet slapped against the brick road, filling the area with venom and manure.

At the forefront of this strange army stood Marianne, her arms spread wide as if in an embrace.

"All for the sake of loooooooooooooooooooooooooove!"

"You... You've gone mad."

Marianne's shout dripped with affection, and as it echoed, Elisabeth spoke in a whisper, her voice strained as though she was enduring a headache. For whatever reason, Marianne's cheeks flushed even redder in embarrassment as she nodded.

Hina held her halberd at the ready, her eyes trained on her foe. She didn't drop her guard as she spoke.

"...I am deeply repulsed by her, and yet, I feel we share a certain affinity. I wonder why that is."

"I'm begging you, Hina—don't follow in her footsteps."

"Oh my, no! That's not what I meant at all, Master Kaito! While I can sympathize with the pain of seeing one's master go astray, and while I understand the strength of the emotions that cause her such madness, I would never dream of being so insolent as to kill my own master. Under such circumstances, it is all the more important for a servant to serve their master with unfettered devotion, to serve their master with every fiber of their being, and to serve their master even at the cost of their own life. For to love is to renounce one's self, and were it for Master Kaito's sake, I would gladly embrace death."

"Hina, in front of you!"

The army of meat-frogs all leaped at once. They paid no heed to the fact that they were crushing one another's tender decaying flesh as they charged for Kaito and Hina. Suddenly, Hina swayed and vanished. She appeared in front of the meat-frogs, waving her halberd.

"How dare you…"

The front-most meat-frog's chest burst with a *splorch*. Offal and venom rained down upon the meat-frogs behind it. Hina shot forward, almost dancing across the corpse as she did a half spin and swung her halberd. She eradicated every frog around her.

She swung her halberd again to dash the venom from its blade, then brought it to a halt.

"…lumps of flesh interfere…"

Hina lowered her center of gravity, then broke into a fierce run. As she passed a Knight's horse, she drove her halberd into it, slashing it in two. Momentum sent the bottom half sailing into the distance, but it eventually toppled to the road. The top portion collapsed where it stood, and the Knight atop it glanced around anxiously.

"...with my lovey-dovey conversation with Master Kaito!"

Hina sent the horse's head flying. When the Knight fell over and landed with his head at her feet, she kicked it off into the distance.

Hina's elegant steps resembled a dance as she returned to Kaito. She then twirled her halberd, sending chunks of flesh flying into the air. She retightened her grasp on the handle and smiled at Kaito.

Her smile was angelic.

"My apologies. To continue our conversation, were it for Master Kaito's sake, I would gladly embrace death. Rest assured: I won't let them lay a single finger on your precious body."

"Th-thanks. That's a huge relief. N-now that I think about it, what's Elisabeth—?"

Stuttering at Hina's intensity, Kaito surveyed the area.

The mass-produced demons were charging at Elisabeth like ominous waves. However, she showed no signs of concern. To the contrary, she swung a spiked iron ball around freely, smashing the demons to bits.

"What exactly are these, Marianne?"

"One of the thirteen demons, one you already defeated. Alternatively, his underlings. Back when they were alive, I took a sample of their blood. Using that as an intermediary, I can summon a portion of their soul and duplicate it. This is the result of placing their twisted souls in temporary shells of meat."

"This is no act of an amateur necromancer. Vlad is surely behind it."

"Indeed. He has been a tremendous aid to me. I had to sacrifice many people to get this far. But it was all for you, young miss. What choice did I have? Those sacrifices were all necessary in order for a weak, ordinary woman like myself to go up against the Torture Princess."

As Marianne spoke, Kaito saw the group of demons re-forming. Their base material was probably human flesh. While this town was full of bones, not a single scrap of flesh remained on any of the corpses. From where was Marianne getting all that meat? His stomach churned just thinking about the quantity of materials her technique must require.

Marianne clasped her silk-gloved hands together, as if in prayer.

"Ah, indeed. I had no choice; I had no choice; I had no choice no choice no choice! I was left with no other choice! In order to become like you, I had no choice but to bear the same sins!"

Blue flames raced alongside her as though in concert with her rising voice. The flames billowed up, as if re-creating the fire that once filled the town, and from them poured an army of Knights.

The Knights charged at Elisabeth. A crowd of new meat-frogs advanced on Kaito and Hina.

"How dare you all show your ugly faces before Master Kaito!"

Hina swung her halberd, taking into account the path the venom would spray before she struck. But when she did, the bones that had been lying around now rose up as a shield to block her attack. The bones scattered, but the meat-frog she'd been aiming at narrowly escaped harm.

"Hina, are you oka—?"

"...Such insolence!"

Hina roared, then drove the sole of her foot into the frog's snout. She pulverized its head, and its body scattered against the ground. The hem of Hina's maid outfit fluttered as she made her graceful landing.

"I thank you for your concern, Master Kaito. What a kind man you are... But that was a trivial matter."

When Kaito looked back at Elisabeth, her circumstances seemed much the same as before.

A number of skeletons were clinging to her iron ball. Even as their bodies shattered, they clutched the spikes and dug their feet into the ground to impede the ball's momentum. Kaito finally realized it. Marianne was planning on using the countless corpses Elisabeth had left to turn this into a battle of resources.

"Ah, can you feel it, young miss? The regrets running across your skin, the anguish boiling in your chest? You are on the verge of being killed by the very innocents you killed long ago. Can you feel it? Can you feel it pounding away at you, young miss, pounding away at your flesh and blood? Can you feel the rage, the hatred, and the sorrow of those you murdered?"

Marianne clutched her abdomen as she cried out with the intensity of an opera singer.

Lances were being pointed at Elisabeth from every direction. She snapped her fingers in irritation.

"Do you understand, young miss? Do you understand that those you killed lived normal lives, lives they wanted to protect? You didn't have the right to kill a single one of them, young miss, not a single one!"

She was clearly unstable. The ecstatic flush vanished from her cheeks. She gripped her chest even tighter, breathing hard, as if to demonstrate her pain as she shed sloppy tears.

"Why, young miss? Why? Why did you do such a terrible thing? Why couldn't you understand how wrong it was?! Young miiiiiiiiiiiiiiiiiiiiiiss?!"

"…Did her heart split in two or something?"

Kaito couldn't help but mumble to himself. Everything Marianne was doing and saying was contradictory. She was gleefully trying to kill Elisabeth out of love yet at the same time tearfully trying to compel her to regret her actions and repent.

"Young miss, why is it, why is it that you can't understand…? I will I will stop you. Doing such a thing will, all the people will cry, I have to kill, young miss, I have to stop her, I have to…"

Kaito finally realized: Marianne's spirit was unraveling. She was being crushed both by the horrible spectacle Elisabeth had forced her to witness long ago and by her own guilt for not having been able to stop it.

"…I, my, I, my young miss, my fault, so…"

What stood before Kaito, Elisabeth, and Hina was nothing more than the shell of a broken woman.

Marianne let out a high-pitched laugh and covered her face. It almost sounded like a scream. The lilies gently swayed atop her hat. Although Elisabeth clicked her tongue, she also whispered softly.

"…What a miserable state you're in, Marianne. I suppose I'm to blame for that."

Suddenly, she stopped walking. Kaito watched her.

Then a skeletal arm reached out and grabbed her. At once, it pulled her into the throng of the dead. The Torture Princess was buried in the bloodlust and the hate of those she had brutally killed.

Loathsome Elisabeth, repulsive Elisabeth, cruel, hideous Elisabeth!

A curse upon you, a curse upon you, a curse, a curse, an eternal curse upon you, Elisabeth!

Kaito felt almost as though he, too, could hear the scathing cries of the dead. He shouted, refusing to lose to them.

"Elisabeth! Quit screwing around and get your ass outta there!"

"Lady Elisabeth, I'm coming!"

Hina shouted, too, then broke into a run. But before she could reach it, the pile of bones began writhing and clattering, driving into Elisabeth's body the same pain they once suffered. Marianne raised her voice once more.

"Do you understand? Have you come to understand, young miss? Young miss, my dear young miss!"

"I've understood that...since the very..."

A small voice leaked out of the pile. Hina, flustered, stopped in her tracks. As she did, the voice exploded out.

"BEGINNINGGGGGGGGGGGGGGGGGGGGGGGG-GGGGGGGGGGGGGGGGGGGGGGGGGGGGGGGGGGGGGG!"

In concert with the enraged voice, chains exploded forth.

The chains clattered as they snaked from Elisabeth. They coiled and spun like a tornado, mowing down the dead with reckless abandon. Bones fractured, snapped, and crumbled.

The maelstrom of chains then spread, blooming like an iron rose. They scraped the ground, struck debris, and smashed the bones to splinters. They thoroughly pulverized all the people she'd once tortured, the people she'd once killed. Upon seeing the chains rage like a many-headed snake, Hina praised her master's master.

"Well done, Lady Elisabeth! I should have expected nothing less. However, this is... Look out! Pardon me, Master Kaito!"

"Hwah!"

Hina returned to him at top speed, then scooped him up in her arms before taking off again. Not a second later, the place where they'd been standing was assaulted by chains. A half-destroyed house appeared in their path, and the chains brought it crumbling down. Ash and charred splinters went flying.

Once the impressive cloud of dust settled, Elisabeth stood alone. She breathed heavily, like a cat with its hair standing on end. The Executioner's Sword of Frankenthal burned in her hand.

Marianne took a step back. The few remaining Knights lined up in front of her. Before they could charge, though, Elisabeth thrust the Executioner's Sword of Frankenthal into the ground.

"Hellhole!"

As she spoke, the earth rumbled. A large cone-shaped cavity yawned in the middle of the road, and the Knights all fell in.

At the bottom of the giant hole, an endless sea of insects wriggled and squirmed. They had lustrous, metallic black shells, and they looked otherworldly. The bugs swarmed the Knights, and their tiny teeth made sickening noises as they chewed on the Knights' rotting flesh. They seemed overjoyed at the generous offering of prey.

"......!"

Marianne slowly backpedaled. But all around her, chains shot out of the ground like serpents. They bound her from head to toe, slim frame, supple breasts, and all.

She hung in the air much like Elisabeth once had. She stared straight at her, as if waiting for an answer to her earlier cries.

Elisabeth stood before her, both hands placed on the hilt of her sword. She bore a serious expression.

"My apologies, Marianne. I've understood that for a long, long time."

Marianne's eyes widened slightly. Elisabeth returned her ashen-blue gaze.

"I had no right to take the light of a single person in this world. Every person I killed led a vigorous life, a life they had every right to carry out as they pleased. They were innocent, and I murdered them. I killed them cruelly, gruesomely, mercilessly, and unreasonably. 'Tis as you say, Marianne. Not even my death will be punishment enough."

Elisabeth's voice was sincere as she tendered her confession. Yet, as she gave it, she spat on the ground. Confessing and acknowledging her sins yet not regretting them in the slightest, Elisabeth stood firm as she made her declaration.

"I became the Torture Princess with full knowledge of what that entailed."

Elisabeth offered no further reasoning.

Her black hair wafted on the hollow wind, a wind that seemed to carry heat from the fire of old, a wind that moaned like the wailing of the vengeful dead.

Loathsome Elisabeth, repulsive Elisabeth, cruel, hideous Elisabeth!

A curse upon you, a curse upon you, a curse, a curse, an eternal curse upon you, Elisabeth!

Taking in all the hatred and the malice of the dead, Elisabeth carried on.

"I shan't ask for forgiveness, nor shall I ask for sympathy. For it is true that I delighted in their screams and bathed in their despair. You should hold me in contempt as you die. Disparage me and curse my name... My apologies, Marianne."

"...Young miss..."

"I intend to follow you shortly. Quite shortly indeed."

Elisabeth's lips betrayed a quiver. For a fleeting second, she wore the face of a defenseless little girl.

She gathered strength in the hand that bore the Executioner's Sword of Frankenthal. Marianne, watching her, shook her head. She pressed her eyes shut, reopened them, then spoke with the gentle demeanor of a tutor.

"Young miss, I know the Executioner's Sword of Frankenthal is a powerful catalyst, capable of summoning chains and torture devices. But I also know that the sword itself was made to allow executioners to behead criminals painlessly before they were put to the stake. A weapon crafted out of kindness. Is that what you intend to kill me with?"

"Indeed, Marianne. With this blade, I shall take the head of a mad, unremarkable woman."

"That won't do, young miss. It's unlike you. You mustn't show even a single person kindness. If you intend to walk down your warped path to the end, you must torture me to death."

Elisabeth's face stiffened a little. As she rebuked Elisabeth, Marianne looked at her with eyes burning with determination.

"If you reject me through pain, kill me through pain, and then the world will finally be free of any who could damage your resolve. If you wish to retain your tyrannical nature now that you've been captured and made the Church's hound, then that is what you must do."

Marianne closed her eyes, then opened them gently. The expression she showed Elisabeth was stern, the childhood teacher within awake at last.

"If you turn a blind eye to even one person, it will weaken your resolve. That's just the way things are."

Elisabeth didn't respond. But Marianne's expression changed once more, from that of a stern instructor to that of an adult speaking to a willful child. Her eyes were full of kindness.

"I loved you from the bottom of my heart, young miss. Even now, I adore you just as much as I did when you were a child."

She smiled gently. Her next words were steeped in sorrow.

"Once you've killed me, I imagine there will be no one left in this world who truly loves you."

"Yes... I will have no one. Not a single person for the rest of eternity."

Elisabeth quietly affirmed Marianne's declaration. Marianne nodded, then inclined her head as if awaiting judgment. Elisabeth let go of the Executioner's Sword of Frankenthal.

Her long, sleek black hair fluttered as Elisabeth looked up at the sky. Her expression was calm. A heavy silence bore down on them. Neither woman, not the one judging nor the one awaiting judgment, moved a hair.

Just then, the space around Kaito froze over.

"...What...the hell?"

The sound of shattering glass faded, and after a few seconds, Kaito realized how odd his surroundings were.

Everything, as far as the eye could see, was frozen over in a light shade of blue. Not just Elisabeth and Hina but the fragments of bone blowing in the wind and the clouds of dust were still as well. He reached his hand out timidly, but there was some sort of transparent film keeping him from touching any of the frozen objects.

"What's going on? Hey, Elisabeth! Hina!"

He called out to them, but it seemed that his voice couldn't reach them, as they didn't respond. In his confusion, he suddenly sensed someone behind him. He spun around in a panic.

"A pleasure to meet you, Sinless Soul."

"A pleasure to meet you, Pure Soul."

Two girls bowed before him, holding the hems of their dresses in polite curtsies. The maid outfits they wore were even more old-fashioned than Hina's. One carried a box tied with a ribbon in an arm, and the other held a clock with a stopped needle. They both had long, draping hair made of tangled gold thread, and for eyes they each bore scuffed-up purple gems. Looking at their artificial parts, Kaito could tell: They weren't human.

The two girls were dolls. They remained expressionless as they spoke, only their lips moving.

"Do you think Elisabeth will kill her?"

"Do you think the Torture Princess can kill her?"

"What? What the hell are you two talking about?"

"What a painful thing it is, to kill a loved one."

"What a sad thing it is, to kill one you adore."

"I mean, you're right. But it's not like I can stop her."

Kaito clenched his fists hard. He didn't know anything about Marianne and Elisabeth's relationship or their bonds. He had no way of knowing what memories they shared or what was currently going through their minds.

The decision rested on Elisabeth's shoulders. And Kaito certainly wouldn't be permitted to weigh in on it, especially not with his limited understanding of the situation. But the maids shook their heads in unison.

"No one said to stop her."

"We said nothing of the sort."

""The question we wish to pose is not about Elisabeth but about you.""

"…What?"

Kaito had no idea what the two were talking about. Who were they anyway?

The maid carrying the box gave a mechanical "Ahem," then slowly stepped forward. Kaito, on his guard, stepped back. But the maid simply unfastened the ribbon, then opened the box and displayed its contents to him with a flourish.

Kaito covered his mouth, assailed by a strong urge to vomit.

"…Rgh—"

Inside the box squirmed a pile of spiders with crow feathers growing all over their bodies. They crawled over one another as they paced about on their eight feathered legs. And there, buried beneath the pile of diminutive horrors, was a baby. Just as he was about to reach his hands into the box of spiders to save it, Kaito gasped.

"It can't be."

"Oh my, did he notice?"

"Indeed, did he understand?"

At a second glance, Kaito noticed the spider legs growing out from the plump baby's waist. The baby had already teethed, and its toothy grin seemed oddly cruel.

A shock ran through Kaito's brain as he comprehended what he saw.

"Is... Is that thing the Earl?"

Now that he thought about it, the Earl had been absent from the group of revived demons who had attacked them a moment ago.

Reeling with disgust, he took a step back. As he did, the maids spoke.

"Marianne possessed the soul of the Earl, as well."

"We placed it in the body of this child."

""As things are, it will grow up to be just like that grotesque man.""

The baby stroked the spiders with its fat hand as one would stroke a pet. A cunning intellect lurked in its eyes, and it grinned contentedly as it looked down upon the spiders.

Kaito raised a fist. But he couldn't convince himself to bring it down. If he'd been facing the original Earl, he would have killed him in a heartbeat. He would no doubt have torn him limb from limb. But even if the creature before him possessed the same nature as the Earl, it was just a baby.

Hitting it wouldn't be enough to kill it. And strangling a baby would make him no better than his father. He forced himself to unclench his fist, then gently rubbed his own pale face.

The maids, having watched him, looked at each other once before nodding.

"Ah, it was too hard a choice to make in the spur of the moment."

"Well, we can wait for him to live up to our expectations."

""This will do for now.""

Suddenly, the maid raised the box in the air. Then, without a shred of hesitation, she threw it hard against the ground.

Panicking, the spiders fled from the cracks in the box. The baby crawled out, crushing the spiders as it went. The maid who previously held the box knocked the baby down with her foot, then stomped on it with all her might.

"Wh—!"

Her strength was inhuman, and the baby's stomach warped before bursting open. Its entrails, structurally different from a human's, came spilling out. The baby convulsed in the pool of its own blue blood for a while before growing still. Kaito found himself at a loss for words, and the maids shrugged.

"Now it's been crushed. Do you feel better?"

"Now it's been dealt with. Do you feel relieved?"

"Why would I—? Well, that's not true. I *do* feel relieved, dammit. God! You guys made that thing in the first place, didn't you? Why would you do something like—?"

"Precisely. We made it. And even though we crushed it, we can still make more."

"As long as Marianne, the necromancer who holds his soul in her womb, lives, we can make as many as we wish."

Upon hearing that, Kaito felt the blood drain from his face. He looked at the baby's mangled corpse. Their being able to produce more of those was a fact he couldn't take lightly.

"Now, here is your question. Will Elisabeth kill her? Or will she not?"

"If she cannot kill her, we intend to snatch Marianne up and produce an army of Earls."

Kaito glanced at Marianne's chain-bound pale face. On it was etched her resolution toward death and her exhaustion toward life. She wasn't the kind of person who should have had to become a necromancer.

"...You mean you're going to exploit her even more? Hasn't she had enough?"

"Until her fragile heart breaks, we intend to mass-produce Earls and release them into the wild."

"Ah, and that scene will play out once more. Countless delightful Grand Guignols will take place."

The maids giggled in unison. Kaito's vision went red with fury.

At the same time, hallucinations of spiders crawled about in his brain. One after another, children screaming their throats raw ran through his mind. Neue cursing his fate, then smiling tearfully. The boy's body being pulled backward and disappearing.

He thought he heard a ghastly scream and the boy's bones snapping. The first person who had ever wished him happiness being brutally killed.

Kaito's mind was painted over with heartache and vengeance. Somewhere in his mind, an odd slamming noise resounded. He looked up slowly. His eyes were opened wide in a manic death glare, and he posed a question to the two maids in a cold voice.

"...You think I'll let you?"

"Your valor is impulsive but splendid nonetheless."

"But we are not the ones you need to face."

The maids clasped the hems of their dresses once more, bending their knees as they curtsied gracefully. The maid who'd been holding the box pointed at Marianne, bound in chains. The other raised her clock.

"Now then, shall we resume?"

"You have only a few seconds to make your choice. Act quickly, if you please."

""Do as you will, but ensure that you have no regrets.""

Then the two disappeared. Color returned to the world. The cold wind blew, and the cloud of dust danced through the air. Elisabeth bit her lip, then raised her hand high.

As she did, Kaito took off at a run.

The maids had told him he had only a few seconds to decide. He didn't have time to wait and see if she would snap her fingers or not. If she didn't, there wouldn't be time to keep the situation from getting ugly.

Kaito had immediately understood what the two had insinuated. His mind was clear, he understood what he needed to do, and he did it without hesitation.

He pulled the Executioner's Sword of Frankenthal out of the ground where it was buried. The blade was remarkably light, possibly due to the magical assistance it offered. Elisabeth turned around. Her crimson gaze clearly meant to question what he was doing, but he ignored it as his body was practically thrown forward. He already knew how unreasonable his actions were.

No matter what I do, Marianne's going to end up dead, either from Elisabeth's torture or from being used up and crippled. Those are the only paths left for her.

Either way, she'd find herself facing Hell. Recognizing that, the reality of her situation helped assuage his guilt as he seized the third unspoken option.

"...Sorry."

Kaito ran Marianne through with the sword.

The magical blade encountered little resistance as it pierced her chest.

"...Wh—?"

Marianne coughed up blood, her eyes wide in surprise. Kaito felt himself perk up as it showered him. Warm blood ran down his cheek. For a second, he didn't realize what he'd just done. Then he choked down the bile welling up in his stomach as he peeled his hands from the sword. His gaze met Marianne's. Kaito looked straight at the woman he'd just killed.

Her face was full of bewilderment. Over and over, Kaito mouthed that he was sorry. For some reason, when she saw that, she smiled tenderly.

"A-ah... My...thanks... Truly...this was...the way..."

Her words were cut short. Still bearing a tranquil expression, her head slumped forward. In astonishment, Kaito turned over her dying words in his head. When he did, a possible end to her final sentence came to mind.

"Wait, did you...?"

Maybe Marianne hadn't wanted to add any further sins to the burden Elisabeth bore. But before he could give the matter much thought, Kaito was sent flying.

"Urgh!"

He'd been kicked hard, and he slid down the road. He tumbled over the gravel and ash before finally crashing into a pile of rubble. The pain that ran across his body was so intense, he was afraid one of his organs had ruptured. Coughing up blood, he looked up.

Elisabeth was standing at the same spot he'd been a moment ago. She gazed at Marianne's corpse, her face devoid of expression. A long moment passed. Then suddenly, Elisabeth grabbed the hilt of the sword piercing Marianne and gave it a yank. Blood gushed from the wound, staining the ground dark.

Elisabeth's black hair fluttered as she turned toward Kaito. Her eyes were narrowed and filled with a dry rage.

"Why act on your own, cur? Based on your answer, you can imagine the punishment that awaits you."

Her heels clicked as she approached. She stopped directly in front of Kaito.

Kaito stared stupidly at the pale hand approaching him. But just before her fingers could reach him, his vision blurred horizontally. Hina had scooped him up, then leaped to the side. She scraped the ground as she landed, carrying him in her right arm and holding the halberd in her left hand at the ready. Elisabeth clicked her tongue.

"Drop it, doll."

"I refuse. You are not my master."

The two glared daggers at each other. Determining that this was not a foe she could contest one-handed, Hina gently set Kaito down and stood in front of him as a shield. Elisabeth pursed her lips coldly.

Trying to prevent a fight, Kaito opened his mouth. But his

breathing was so ragged, he couldn't speak well. He tried his best to gather strength in his wounded chest.

"H-hey, you two, cut it—"

But the moment he'd finally gathered the strength to speak, he realized that the space around him had frozen once again.

Even with his vision blurred from the pain in his abdomen, he could make out the two maids standing in front of him. One of them was wearing shoes stained with the blood of a baby, and the other held her clock. They turned their scuffed purple eyes toward Kaito without a word. The next moment, their fair faces clicked and contorted into expressions that were anything but natural.

The maids wore broken, hideous smiles. They gracefully bowed once again.

"You passed, Sinless Soul."

"Our master calls for you."

Humming contentedly, the maids grabbed Kaito's limp shoulders. He was helpless to resist as they pulled him away. As they dragged him along, he weakly turned to look over his shoulder. After the three of them had traveled a fixed distance, the frozen-blue world suddenly sprang back to life.

"Hmm? ...Kaito?"

"Mas— Master Kaito? This can't be! Master Kaito, where are you?!"

Elisabeth and Hina noticed Kaito's disappearance and surveyed their surroundings. He wasn't that far away from them. He stared at them, begging them to notice him. Hina turned in his direction. But then a sound rang out.

Grrrrrrrrr, grrrrrrrrrrrr, grrrrrrrrrrr.

As if to block their view, a deep-black darkness coalesced and swallowed the light. As it growled, the darkness formed fine, rippling muscles and sleek black fur.

Before long, it had taken the form of a first-class hound. Crimson hellfire burned in its eyes.

The Kaiser had arrived, and the air itself froze in awe.

"Gah-ha-ha-ha, heh-heh-ha-ha, gah-ha-ha-ha."

He laughed at the two of them in a voice that sounded almost human.

That hopeless scene was the last thing Kaito saw before his consciousness faded.

Elisabeth Le Fanu

The Torture Princess. A beautiful woman who massacred her people, her acts of torture even extending to the nobles. She is set to be executed. The Church orders her to punish sinners who contracted with demons, saying, "Until the day of your death, try to do some good at least."

6
Kaito's Decision

Kaito reflected on just how miserable his life had been.

People kept calling him a Sinless Soul, but he certainly didn't feel like one. On the contrary, as he'd just committed his first murder in this world. Even though he'd been complicit in murders before, such as helping clean up bodies, this was the first time he'd ever stabbed someone with a sword.

His new life had been a mess. He'd born witness to unspeakably horrible sights and been tortured for nonsensical reasons. He'd been forced to cut off his own hand and carve deep wounds in his own chest. But despite all that, he'd also had some experiences he didn't want to forget.

Someone had wished him happiness. Someone had promised to protect him.

He'd had to dig through metaphorical mud, chunks of metal tearing at his flesh, but he'd finally received those blessings.

For most people, small comforts like those were a constant in their day-to-day lives, trivial motes of warmth that hardly bore mention. But it had taken Kaito until after his death to receive them.

Because of that, Kaito thought something for the first time.

He definitely wasn't a Sinless Soul, and the things he'd seen had been hellish. But even so... In spite of all that...

★   ★   ★

This second life he'd had forced upon him wasn't a bad one.

Perhaps there had been meaning in the resurrection of a pitiful creature like himself after all.

Of course, he'd never share these thoughts with anyone.

When he opened his eyes, Kaito found himself seated on an extravagant chair. His surroundings were dimly lit, and the edges of his vision faded into darkness. He brushed against his chair's expertly crafted armrests as he surveyed the room.

Wait, where am I? What am I doing here?

A pearl-gray tablecloth extended out before him. On the table lay an assortment of foods on silver buffet platters. The food was so colorful, it almost looked like it was made of wax.

There were a number of hors d'oeuvres, from a translucent gelled oyster dish and a vividly orange marinated salmon to a broad selection of pâtés. For entrees, there was a golden-brown pig roast, a vegetable quiche, and an aromatic lobster chowder. There were also fruits drizzled in honey, a cake covered in crushed almonds, and an olive-brown pudding adorned with berries.

The table was absolutely packed with fragrant foods. Flames illuminated them from atop red candlesticks, flickering as they cast their light on the banquet that looked too good to be true. But despite the meal's splendor, nobody was partaking of the spread.

The silhouette of a man sat at the head of the table.

★   ★   ★

He wore a silk shirt with a cravat. His coat was decorated with silver thread, and he declined to remove it as he ate. The man ignored the buffet platters, instead eating from a single pure-white dinner plate.

Upon the porcelain dish was a slab of meat with blood dripping from it. The raw liver didn't even look seasoned. The man cut thin slices of the meat and carried them to his mouth with his fork.

The darkness was broken up only by the candlelight and the soft sound of dishes clinking.

Kaito immediately recognized the man's crimson eyes, silky black hair, and beautiful, androgynous features.

The man, Vlad, bore a striking resemblance to Elisabeth.

But...why? Why'd they bring me straight to the final boss, of all people?

Confused, Kaito took stock of his body. The pain in his abdomen hadn't gone away, but he could move his arms and legs freely. He wasn't bound, nor did there appear to be any manner of magical restraints.

Kaito looked at Vlad, hoping he would drop his guard. Vlad simply continued eating in silence. He seemed engrossed in the meat, as if it was the sole thing on his mind. It was unclear if his guard was down or not. Kaito then turned away from the table to check out the room. However, he couldn't make out many details. Any part of the room that was even slightly removed from the candlelight was shrouded in darkness.

I can't even tell where the entrance is. That's not good.

Kaito choked back his impatience and frustration and calmed his breathing. He had to keep cool. But the feral aroma the smoke from the candles emitted set his nerves on edge. It evoked the image of that black dog, its eyes burning with hellfire.

That reminds me—are Elisabeth and Hina all right?
"Hmm? Caught your attention, has it?"

Kaito looked up with a start. Vlad, no longer eating, wore a surprised expression on his face. Kaito hadn't expected him to sound so young. Unsure of how to respond, Kaito elected to remain silent.

"My invitation was rather abrupt, I'll admit. No doubt you're rather confused at the moment. My apologies."

Vlad nodded to himself, then snapped his fingers. Darkness and azure flower petals spiraled in front of Kaito, and a bowl of water appeared. The water's surface formed a mirror, then projected a distant scene.

Kaito's eyes widened as he looked at it.

"Elisabeth... Hina..."

Elisabeth and Hina were making their way up the slope to the castle, fighting off a colossal black dog as they ran.

Hina swung her halberd, knocking the black dog off its feet. However, her blade couldn't pierce the dog's thick fur. Elisabeth sent countless stakes flying toward its back, but they all simply bounced off. The dog's jaw bore down on her, and she bound it with conjured chains. But although she restrained it, she couldn't deal a decisive blow.

"Damn you. To think that you would resist my torture devices this well. Truly, you bear the Kaiser's name well."

Elisabeth spat a mouthful of blood on the roadside. Her sharp intent to kill hadn't been dulled. But try as she might to hide it, her crimson eyes were stained with frustration.

Placing both hands on the table, Kaito reflexively shouted out: "Elisabeth!"

"Don't you think she's being a bit impatient? As I see it, Elisabeth is more volatile than a powder keg. Only a fool would try using brute force to subdue the Kaiser. Although to that point, I suppose trying to fight him in the first place was a mistake in and of itself."

Vlad shrugged, his voice filled with the intimacy of one describing their willful child. He gracefully brought the last piece of meat to his mouth. After wiping his bloodstained lips, he gestured with his fork to the bowl Kaito was staring at.

"The Kaiser is the highest ranked among all the demons we summoned, the apex of what man can invoke. Even Elisabeth, the famed Torture Princess, won't be able to kill him quite that easily. It would bear poorly upon the Kaiser's name if she could. And he has his pride as a first-rate hound to consider, as well. The leader of the fourteen is in a league all his own."

That was the kind of foe Elisabeth and Hina were fighting. Kaito clenched his fists hard. But then he noticed something out of place.

"Wait, hold up a minute. The demon's over there, but you're right here. Does that mean you summoned the Kaiser, but you didn't fuse with him?"

"Precisely. You likely heard it from Elisabeth already, but I acted as the intermediary to materialize the Kaiser into this world. In a sense, the two of us are as one. Normally, it would have been prudent to merge with him for the sake of my own safety. But I'd rather not abandon the pleasure that comes of having a human body, nor do I much care to have my form reduced to such a hideous state—they are laughably hideous, are they not?"

Vlad chuckled. With a frankness that bordered on cruelty, he laughed at his fellow demons. Kaito was reminded of the time Elisabeth had instructed him to laugh at an underling.

Kaito shook his head, then continued asking questions.

"So that means you're flesh and blood, right? And if I kill you, the Kaiser will die with you."

"Quite so! A rather foolish thing to ask me, though, don't you think? You seem surprisingly foolhardy, so I'll advise a bit of caution—you can't kill me."

Vlad delivered this statement with total apathy. He took his napkin and wiped more blood from his lips.

"Elisabeth might stand a chance, but... Much like her, I am no ordinary human."

Azure flower petals and darkness gathered around his fingertips. He let go of his napkin, and it unraveled. The thread drew a spiral in the air, then suddenly burst into flames. White ash fluttered gently to the table.

Watching him handle the darkness and blue petals, Kaito realized something. This man was close to what Elisabeth would be if she contracted with a demon, just like in Clueless's example.

"So why'd you bring me here? Are you going to use me as a hostage?"

"...Forgive me. You don't seem to be joking but rather laboring under a misapprehension... Tell me, do you honestly believe that you would have any value as a hostage?"

"Oh, hell no. I'm just a benchwarmer. I doubt Elisabeth gives a damn whether I live or die."

"I agree. I invited you here because I have a certain proposal for you."

Vlad nodded again in a show of near-innocent frankness. But his face then turned serious, and he crossed his hands as he looked at Kaito.

"I wish to adopt you as my son and mold you into a second Elisabeth."

"Hard pass."

Kaito immediately refused, not waiting to learn what Vlad meant by "a second Elisabeth."

Despite his confusion, he was sure of his answer. The instant the idea of being the Kaiser's contractor's adopted son came up, refusing was the only reasonable choice. Vlad bore a confused expression, but he continued.

"Oh, Elisabeth. My dearest beloved Elisabeth. She was my first daughter, and she was my masterpiece. Her only flaw was that she surpassed perfection. She matured even faster than I expected, but in the end, she severed all ties with me. I want to replace her. For all I have attained, for all I have yet to attain, I need a successor."

"But why would you pick me of all people? It really makes no sense."

"What I see in you is the potential to surpass even her. I heard a bit from Clueless, but your death was unspeakably cruel despite having committed no sin worthy of such a fate, correct? You understand pain, yet you remain calm in the face of it. On the other hand, you react strongly toward those you hate. Your passion and your composure counterbalance each other."

"I don't know if I'd go that far. I feel like there's a pretty big gap between reality and what you think of me."

"Is there? I daresay the gap is quite small—I believe I can expect great things from those who know pain but can still kill others if it meets their needs."

Vlad snapped his fingers. The blond maids from before appeared behind him. They blinked their scuffed purple eyes, then bowed gracefully. Kaito, taken aback, glared at the two.

Vlad, showing no indication of whether or not he'd picked up on Kaito's hostility, continued, his voice almost musical.

"Above all else, you were murdered and had everything taken from you. And those who have been taken from have a right to take from others in turn. They are, if nothing else, prepared to accept that they have that right. A deep *hunger* is required if one wishes to harness the pain of others. For if one's hunger—one's *desire*—is shallow, they will eventually be consumed by it. You need a certain *capability*—the capability to wear the tyrant's mantle as if it was the role you were born to play."

Vlad's performance was that of a poet, and his analysis of Kaito was that of a scholar.

Kaito struggled desperately to avoid being taken in by Vlad's words. The candles flickered, and Vlad's utterances echoed like an incantation. If he kept listening, Kaito felt that his consciousness might drift away. He needed to avoid losing sight of himself. Kaito had no desire to become like Elisabeth. He doubted he'd even be able to.

The words coming from the man in front of him were nothing but the ravings of a lunatic.

"Ever since she was a child, Elisabeth was exposed to an unreasonable fear of death. Her pain and her fear molded her into the finest work of art. I wish to make you into my second work, into my successor. I admit that wanting a son for having lost a daughter is a rather simple conception, but so be it. What do you say?"

"Hard pass. And quit your babbling; you make me sick."

"Ah, a spirited answer! But do listen just a while longer. You won't regret it."

Vlad was unperturbed. He looked at Kaito the way someone would inspect a mischievous child. Or perhaps it was closer to a breeder, impressed by the strength of a puppy's bark.

"I don't intend to look down on you like Clueless did. And I'm not trying to simply take your future for free. That wouldn't be right... Although now that I say it out loud, I suppose it's a bit odd for me to be talking about right and wrong."

"What're you offering? Elisabeth's and Hina's safety?"

"Heavens no! What makes you think I would give you any say in regard to my daughter? The Kaiser and I will settle things with my beloved daughter, with my beloved, adorable, foolish, loathsome Elisabeth. For that is what love is. Know your place, child—that girl is my, Vlad Le Fanu's, beloved daughter."

For a second, a cold light burned in Vlad's crimson eyes. He strode to Kaito's side, then ran one of his black nails through the bowl of water. Elisabeth's figure blurred.

"Don't think for a moment that you have a place in our relationship."

The glare directed at Kaito lasted only an instant. Then Vlad smiled yet again.

"Besides! What I have to offer you is something much more wonderful, something I think you'll find much more important. You see, my skill in magic surpasses Elisabeth's, and connecting to other worlds is hardly a challenge for me."

Vlad puffed up his chest with pride. His face was so pleased, he looked like a child inviting a friend to come play with him. Despite speaking of adopting others, Vlad himself possessed a certain childishness to him. But all of a sudden, a cruel smile carved its way across Vlad's face. Seeing that expression, Kaito came to a realization.

Fused or not, this man was unmistakably a demon.

And demons wedged their way into the cracks in the hearts of men.

"It seems your father ran into some trivial problems the other day and was drowned at sea. I can summon him and give him to you as a toy."

When he heard those words, Kaito's heart stopped.

"...Wait, you're telling me... You're telling me that asshole *died*?"

Before he realized it, Kaito was standing. His chair tumbled over behind him and landed with a crash. The bowl shook, and the image in the water blurred. But Kaito didn't have the composure to pay attention to any of that.

He felt as though someone had taken a hammer to his skull. A moment later, a sense of emptiness overtook him. It was like his chest had gone hollow and his heart had shattered.

That was how surprised and astonished he was at Vlad's statement.

That man had died. That man who seemed like no matter what happened, he'd live forever. Fuck.

"Oh, that he did. Congratulations—your father died! Perhaps

this is karma at work... Heh, as the bona fide personification of evil, is it contradictory of me to say that? Well, who cares if it's contradictory? What a pleasant result! Now then, what will you do?"

"What will I do...? I mean, he's dead, so..."

"What did I just say? I can bring him back and give him to you as a toy! If you desire revenge for your untimely demise, I recommend nodding. After all, you have no need to hide that from me or be embarrassed."

Vlad nodded repeatedly to demonstrate his understanding and affection. He showed Kaito an innocent smile.

He bore an expression of one inviting another to play a cruel game as he continued.

"Wouldn't it feel *good* to spill his guts, scrape out his lungs, and wring his neck?"

He couldn't afford to lend an ear to Vlad's cajolery. Those were the words of a demon. But even knowing that, Kaito could feel something bubbling up from the cracked depths of his heart. He couldn't deny those sublime dregs of emotion.

He could tear out his father's viscera, then ignore his pleas for mercy as he ruthlessly beat him to death. Just imagining it filled him with satisfaction. Surely, putting it into action would be even more exhilarating.

If he did that, he could finally throw off the fear and hatred that bound him like shackles.

Surely that was worth throwing the rest of his life away.

"Give me...some time to think it over."

Kaito finally managed to choke out those words. It felt like spitting up blood. He was trembling all over, his giddiness so strong, it resembled terror. Vlad nodded magnanimously.

"Take your time. We have plenty of it. Well, you do, at least."

Hearing that, Kaito turned his empty eyes to the water's surface. A sharp silver flash ran diagonally across the view.

"...*Tch!*"

A massive executioner's sickle swung down upon the dog's neck. But the dog blocked it with its jaw and bit down hard enough to shatter it. The maid was still swinging her halberd, but her clothes were covered in rips and tears.

"*Master—— Master—— Master—— Master——where are you?!*"

Sparing no concern for her own wounds or condition, she frantically shouted for someone else.

That's... I'm...

Watching her, Kaito realized there was an emotion he was supposed to feel. But although he understood this necessity, he didn't know what emotion it was. He was in a state of shock, and his mind wasn't able to properly parse the scene before his eyes.

The scene he was witnessing felt like it was taking place in another world. It was like his soul alone had returned to that room he was strangled in, that room he died in.

Unsure of what to do, Kaito reached toward the water like a toddler.

The water engulfed his trembling fingertips.

The mirrorlike surface of the water shattered, and it projected nothing more.

✳

"This will be your room, Master Kaito. Please make yourself at home as you think over your decision."

The speaker was a new, third maid holding a lantern in one hand. She bowed.

As she looked up, her dented pearl eyes glittered. She seemed to be of an older make, as her cheek was beginning to crumble. Kaito nodded, and the maid turned around and left for the dark hallway. The creaking of her loose left ankle faded into the distance.

Now alone, Kaito scanned the dingy room in surprise.

"…Wait, is this the same room?"

This should have been his first time here, yet he remembered this room.

Upon the square room's walls hung yellow wallpaper, so degraded you could just barely make out its floral design. The cute plaster sculptures by the window were covered in ash, and the once-white furniture was filthy as well. However, the metal handles on the chest of drawers were just as vibrant as ever. The chest itself had once been decorated with dolls and stuffed animals, but perhaps in deference to the fact that Kaito was a boy, it now bore a hunting rifle and a model rocking horse. A crushed mat lay atop the spiderweb-ridden four-poster bed. The mattress was covered in a heap of flowing blankets.

Dry bloodstains were splattered all over the fluffy blankets. After taking in the whole scene, Kaito nodded.

"Yeah, this really is Elisabeth's old room."

This was the real-life counterpart to the phantom room he'd stumbled into when he got lost in the Treasury.

★   ★   ★

The door he'd found in the Treasury had most likely used the memories from this room and materialized them within its magical space. The actual room was much dirtier than its phantom counterpart, but its design was almost identical. Vlad must have replaced the things Elisabeth had taken from here, returning the master-less room close to its original form. One more example of his bizarre fixation on her. The fact that he'd accounted for Kaito in spite of that and decorated the room for a boy was almost comical.

"…Heh."

Suddenly, everything seemed hilarious to Kaito. A spasm of intense laughter rocked his chest. He couldn't help it. Everything was just so amusing. He opened his mouth wide and laughed as hard as he could.

"Ha-ha-ha, ha-ha-ha-ha, ah-ha-ha-ha-ha-ha!"

His abdomen cramped, and tears poured out of his eyes. But no matter how much it hurt, he just kept laughing. Everything, from his father's pitiful death to his current situation, was comical beyond belief.

And it was all such bullshit.

Wham!

Kaito suddenly stopped laughing and punched the wall. His bone cracked, and a sharp pain ran up his arm. Even so, he re-clenched his fist. Blood dripped down the wall. His finger was broken, but he punched the wall again and again. He yelled, striking the wall as if possessed.

"He died. That asshole died. After torturing so many people to death, he ended up getting himself killed. Serves that bastard right. But what, is that supposed to make me feel better?! Is that supposed to make me forgive him?! Fuck that—I wanna kill him myself!"

Kaito punched the wall especially hard. His little finger was on the outside of his fist, and it snapped loudly. Even though his mind was steeped in vengeance and hatred, his usual sense of cold composure didn't come. He lashed out in tears, like a child throwing a temper tantrum. He heaved a ragged breath, slammed his forehead into the wall, and mumbled something in a hollow voice.

"But a dead person killing their dead killer... Man, nothing makes sense anymore..."

His tone was full of self-deprecation. He smiled a hollow smile. After a while, he pulled his forehead from the bloodstained wall. He looked around, as if searching for someone who could help him.

His gaze settled on the bed.

"...Elisabeth."

A vision of Elisabeth in her younger days floated before his weary eyes.

The frail, beautiful girl sat half-buried beneath the sea of blankets. She stared at Kaito, her vacant eyes devoid of life. That beauty of hers was the one thing that had never changed.

Kaito grimaced childishly as he asked the young Elisabeth a question.

"Hey, what the hell happened to you? What was it that made you the way you are?"

The vision didn't answer. But Kaito kept asking, practically screaming at it.

"Dammit, Elisabeth! Why'd you choose to become the Torture Princess?!"

It was the question he'd often wondered about and the question he'd never asked her.

Why *had* she become the Torture Princess? What reasons did she have; what hatred did she harbor? Or had she not had any reason at all? Unsurprisingly, the vision didn't explain anything.

After all, she was nothing more than an illusion that Kaito's mind had conjured up due to stress. Kaito knew that. But he implored her nevertheless, and then she simply faded away.

"Ha-ha-ha, ha-ha-ha-ha, ah-ha-ha-ha-ha-ha!"

Kaito began laughing again. He laughed like a madman, laughing and laughing and convulsing with laughter. He punched the wall. His bloodstained fingers made horrible noises as he peeled them off the wall, and he found himself blinking back tears.

Then, all of a sudden, his confusion cleared. No more tears welled up in his eyes. His tantrum ended abruptly. His mind as clear as a still lake, he came to a conclusion.

No matter how much he laughed, this pain would never fade.

He had been stricken down in a manner most foul.

That one fact was his everything.

The maid with the dented pearl eyes was standing by in the hallway.

"Master Vlad is waiting for you in the dining room, sir."

Following her lead, Kaito found himself in the dining room once more. Vlad still sat alone at the head of the table. Unlike

Elisabeth, he didn't seem to take dessert, instead choosing to sip at a glass of wine after having finished his meal. Watching Vlad rock his glass from side to side, Kaito spoke.

"I've made up my mind. Let me kill my dad with my own hands. Even with him dead, I can't forgive him."

"A splendid decision, if I do say so myself. None would deny that you have a right to revenge. Exercising it seems wholly reasonable."

Vlad set his glass down, and he spoke in a warm voice carefully crafted to wash away Kaito's guilt. His face bore no signs of surprise. That was the answer he'd been expecting. And why wouldn't it be? The reason he wanted Kaito as a son was surely because he understood that Kaito was a prisoner of his own hatred.

Kaito softly clenched his aching fist. He wavered a little, then made his follow-up request.

"Before that, though, just once... I won't ask you to let me see your daughter, Elisabeth. But...can I at least say good-bye to Hina?"

"...Hina? Ah, that puppet I left behind without turning it on. I'm surprised you took such a fancy to it. Are you fond of playing with dolls? If you wish, I can have one just like it prepared for you... Or rather, one tuned specifically to your tastes."

"She's not a puppet. And she can't be replaced. Hina is Hina."

Kaito closed his eyes, thinking back to the warm sensation of her arms holding him tight. Her silver hair and adoring smile flickered beneath his eyelids. But then he opened his eyes, erasing the image.

"We only spent a little time together, but I'm indebted to her. Oh, and one other thing. Call off the Kaiser's attack while I'm saying good-bye to Hina. It seems unfair to make Elisabeth fight him alone."

"I must admit I have difficulty comprehending how one could feel indebted to a doll. And if you wished to betray me, this would certainly be a convenient arrangement for you... But this is a special occasion. As my one and only successor, I shall grant you this sole indulgence."

Vlad nodded and gave the pair of gold-haired maids an order. They carried the clock with them as they headed outside. Vlad spoke boastfully as he watched them go.

"That clock is a magical apparatus. It can pull those without magic resistance from the flow of time and space. You yourself saw space halt around you, no? But nobody else was removed from the proper flow of time. The maids, the ones using the device, could have killed you whenever they pleased within that space yet would be unable to so much as lift a finger against Elisabeth outside it. To be blunt, it's a tool designed for weaklings. But I wonder how that automaton will fare. Normally, it would have little effect, but given her wounded state, who knows? Now then, would you care for some wine while we wait?"

"I'm good."

"How cold. I myself find life more enjoyable when it's accompanied by liquor."

Rejecting Vlad's offer, Kaito plopped himself down on a nearby seat. He ignored the food before him and clasped his bloody hands. Vlad gave a light shrug, then lifted his glass.

They remained that way as they waited, time seeming to slow to an agonizing crawl. Eventually, the door to the dining room swung open. Two pairs of footsteps drew near, as well as the sound of something being dragged. Kaito peered in the direction of the noise, and his eyes widened.

"...Hina!"

"There was no need for us to subdue it. It was just lying in the rubble."

"It seems that Elisabeth judged it a hindrance and left it behind."

"That girl, making sure it didn't fight to the point of breaking. Elisabeth did always have her gentle moments. It seems the doll won't be of much use if your plan was to tell it to take Elisabeth and flee from the Kaiser."

Hearing the maids' reports, Vlad cast a sidelong glance at Kaito and laughed at him. Kaito frantically rose from his seat.

The maids were propping Hina up by her shoulders. Her clothes had been shredded, as had her humanlike skin. It didn't seem like she would have trouble walking. Yet, she refused to let go of her halberd.

"...Master...Kaito... Oh...Master Kaito, where...are...?"

As she muttered the single-minded phrase, she looked up, her tangled silver hair swaying. As her vacant emerald eyes landed on Kaito, they widened, and a jovial light flashed within them.

"...Master Kaito!"

Hina shook off the maids, then dropped the halberd she'd been clutching. As she reached out her arms, she seemed to have forgotten her pain entirely. Kaito paused. His plan to entrust Hina with a message and save Elisabeth had gone off the rails, but he was still planning on betraying them. He had no right to be hugged by her.

"Master Kaito! Oh, I'm so, so glad that you're unharmed."

"This is good-bye, Hina. You have to head back to the castle without me."

Hina had been about to rush toward him, but upon hearing his words, she stopped dead in her tracks. She looked like she'd been stabbed in the heart from behind. After a few seconds, she straightened herself out, then looked straight at Kaito.

She softly pressed her hand against her chest, steadied her breathing, then spoke.

"Master Kaito, do you find some aspect of me inadequate, perhaps?"

"Hina, what are you—?"

"If there is, would you permit me to be rude enough to ask what it is? I will repair it. I am but a simple fool, unwitting as to my own failure, but if you give me a chance to fix my mistake, nothing could make me happier. I beg you for clemency."

"No, no, that's not it. You haven't done anything wrong."

Kaito hadn't expected Hina's reaction, and he hastily corrected her. She appeared perplexed.

"If that is the case…then perhaps, have you come to hate me? Can you no longer bear the sight of my face? Do you no longer wish to have someone like me by your side? If that is what the problem is, then I will take my face and, with Lady Elisabeth's aid, reconstruct it so as to better meet your—"

"You're wrong, Hina. There's nothing wrong with you, nothing at all. I just chose to follow this guy."

"Master Kaito… You mean…Vlad?"

Hina looked at the person Kaito was pointing to in bewilderment. Kaito nodded.

"I can't say it's my first choice. But even if I have to stand on the side that hurts others, there's something I need to do. And he's the only one who can make it happen for me."

Kaito tried to explain himself. Hina's expression made her seem like an abandoned puppy, and he had to turn away.

There wasn't a single thing wrong with her. Although he was

betraying her, he didn't want to be the reason she wore such a pained expression. But he didn't have the luxury of being able to keep her by his side.

Right now, she was unfit for combat. If she would just give up on him, Vlad would probably let her go.

After all, their relationship was the result of him accidentally starting her up. If she could just forget about him and find a new master, she should at least be able to spend her days happily and peacefully.

If nothing else, that's what he wanted to believe.

"Just forget about your configured lover, and after you get back, you can live your life freely. I'll have Elisabeth…or, rather, Vlad set it up so you can forget me and arrange a new config—"

"Please don't make light of me, Master Kaito."

"Huh?"

She interrupted Kaito, her voice cold and pointed. She'd never shown such anger toward him before. She took a short breath, exhaled, and straightened herself up in a dignified manner.

"I may have the preconfigured heart of an automaton, but it is still mine and mine alone. The moment I chose you as my master, and you chose me, I decided to dedicate my life and my love to you and no one else. I live because I wish to live for your sake, and I break because I wish to be broken. I have no intention of serving another master. Even if my noble master was to order it, I cannot allow you to deny that fact."

"…Hina…"

"Why do you choose to serve a man such as him?"

"Sorry. I'm gonna follow him. Even if I have to give Vlad everything I hold dear, I'm going to kill my father!"

Before he realized it, Kaito was yelling. As if in response to his unstable thoughts, anger and bloodlust welled up within his heart, and the suffering he'd once felt returned to him. He clenched his teeth, panting like an animal.

The harshness immediately faded from Hina's face and was replaced, in an instant, by understanding. She should have had no way of knowing his past, but she seemed to have sensed something, as she gently asked him a question.

"Will that... Will that bring you happiness?"

"Huh? ...Happiness?"

"Will it?"

"Uh, well, probably."

Overwhelmed by Hina's earnest tone, Kaito nodded. But he had no idea if the act would bring him happiness. To the contrary, homicide was about as far removed as an act could be from something as idyllic as "happiness." But all he had to do was kill his father, and the torrent of muddy hatred flowing through his heart should vanish.

Hearing his response, Hina beamed.

"Thank goodness."

"Huh?"

Kaito was surprised, once again, by her response. For some reason, Hina was nodding in relief. She laid her hands on her chest with a satisfied expression, like a mother understanding her child's happiness.

"Even back at the castle, you never once smiled from the heart, Master Kaito... I was so very worried for you. If this choice will grant you happiness, then there is nothing more for me to say. With a heart full of joy, I shall support you on your path."

"Wait, Hina, you were worried about me all this time?"

"Your happiness is my happiness, Master Kaito. A single,

supreme happiness… I understand. As per your wishes, I will now suspend all functions."

"Wh—?!"

Her unexpected proclamation caused Kaito's eyes to widen. That wasn't what he wanted at all. Hell, the whole reason for this farewell was because he wanted Hina to live a long life.

Kaito grabbed her shoulders. She calmly returned his gaze.

"Hina, quit talking nonsense! Why would you have to shut down?!"

"If you say you no longer have need of me, Master Kaito, then why should I keep on living? Lady Elisabeth does not wish to flee, and I am simply a burden. Please put your mind at ease. If you say this will bring you happiness, then I will gladly return my body to that of a mere doll."

"Cut it out—I'm begging you. Please. I don't want you to die. Can't you think this over?"

"How kind you are… What a truly kind and compassionate man you are. Although I am unworthy of such sentiment, I will accept it nonetheless. But my life is by your side, and the moment you no longer needed me, it came to an end. You needn't feel guilt about this. My work is complete, so instead, please send me off with a smile."

Hina smiled. Her voice rang with a resolute sense of pride, one that far surpassed Kaito's ability to comprehend. No matter what he said, he doubted that her resolve would waver. When he realized that, his hands loosened. Hina took a step back and clasped the hem of her maid uniform. Her silver hair gently swayed as it glittered in the candlelight. She lowered her injured leg and gave a lovely bow.

"And with that, Master Kaito, I take my leave. Within the

hour, unless you find yourself once more in need of me, I shall enter my eternal slumber. You have my sincerest thanks. Allowing me to be by your side...and graciously permitting me to be your lover made me happier than you could possibly imagine."

When Hina expressed how happy she'd been in the short time they'd spent together, her voice contained no traces of falsehood, just fervent gratitude. She bowed deeply, then continued.

"With a heart full of love and gratitude, I welcome death... Please excuse me."

She finished her bow, picked up her halberd, and used it to prop up her body as she walked. The maids went to lend a hand, but she shook them off and left the dining room alone. Her resolute figure soon receded into the darkness.

Standing frozen in place, Kaito watched her leave.

As he did, he recalled Marianne and Elisabeth's exchange.

"Once you've killed me, I imagine there will be no one left in this world who truly loves you."

"Yes... I will have no one. Not a single person for the rest of eternity."

He felt as though he had just lost something precious without having ever realized just how important it was.

He remained motionless. But before he could process his profound sense of loss, Vlad called out from behind him.

"I have to ask, just for the record. Did I witness a miracle a moment ago? A miracle such as your plaything's lofty words washing away your age-old grudge, leaving you with a cleansed spirit and ready to live happily ever after?"

"...Don't worry about it. Just summon my fucking dad already."

Kaito spat out his words. Vlad nodded, then snapped his fingers.

The maids quickly rolled in a cart designed to carry food, as if they'd been waiting impatiently for this. The top of the cart was covered in a silver lid, which the maids promptly removed.

Upon the cart lay a doll clad in gray clothes. It had no hair, eyes, or mouth.

The ball-jointed doll's skin was pale, and its construction looked so plain that it was difficult to imagine it housing a soul. Vlad took a knife from the table, spun it by its hawk-insignia handle, and brought it to a sharp stop. He then forcefully plunged it more than halfway through his wrist.

The cut severed an artery, and blood gushed forth across the tablecloth and dripped onto the floor. The blood coalesced, seeming almost alive, and began painting a complicated design on the floor, a different design than the teleportation circle Kaito was familiar with.

While that was happening, Vlad gave a brief scowl. His arm, hidden in his sleeve until then, shone crimson with divine glyphs. The Church's shackles were burned into his skin. It seemed that when he used magic, they caused him even more pain. However, his expression quickly returned to neutral.

"My words bear no lies. My words bear no falsehoods. My words bear no untruths. His soul ferries between worlds. On Earth he calls out, his body in tatters. In the ether he finds his form once more."

Vlad muttered something in a low voice. In concert with his chant, the summoning circle on the ground flickered.

As the light grew stronger, the atmosphere in the room began to change.

"*La* (become)— *La* (traverse)— *La* (become)— *La* (return)— *La* (become)—"

The air grew dry and sharp, as if thousands of pieces of glass were flying through it. A formless radiance danced on the tip of Kaito's nose, and he tracked it with his gaze. The edges of his vision were full of images that were most definitely from another world.

Highways, cars, crowds, billboards, rivers, schools. All of them scenes from the world he'd left behind.

They refracted with a rainbow of colors, filling the dark room with a strange light.

"You should close your eyes for the rest. Staring at the light for too long would drive ordinary men mad. You wouldn't want to have your soul sucked out, would you?"

Hearing Vlad's warning, Kaito frantically squeezed his eyes shut. Still, the rainbow light burned into his retinas. As he turned toward the darkness to ward off the light, memories of the events leading up to now flashed through his mind.

As if fleeing from the strange light, Kaito sank into the depths of a sea of memories.

A beautiful girl with fluttering dark hair spoke, her tone of voice often waxing between malice and pride.

"I am the Torture Princess, Elisabeth Le Fanu."
"I am the proud wolf and the lowly sow."
"You and I—we are fated to die, forsaken by all of creation."

★   ★   ★

A pretty doll with fluttering silver hair gave a smile full of kindness and affection.

"Everything is going to be okay, Master Kaito. No matter what happens, I'll protect you."
"With a heart full of love and gratitude, I welcome death."

A red-haired boy gave a pained smile, his voice trembling in confusion as he answered.

"I was just hoping you could find happiness in this world."

In the end, he hadn't been able to fulfill Neue's wish.

When he realized that, his chest began pounding violently. His heart ached, and it hurt to breathe. *Are you really okay with this?* a calmer, more composed part of himself asked. *Will this really leave you without regrets?*

Shut up, shut up… Even if it doesn't, I still have to—
As he tried to respond, he heard Vlad's voice.

"…It is done."
And Kaito opened his eyes.

"…H-huh?"
The man standing before him was unmistakably his father.

⋆   ⋆   ⋆

The stern, unshaven man looked about anxiously. He tore at his unkempt black hair, and his eyes darted around the room like a chameleon's. Kaito recognized that face. He recognized that conspicuous hooknose. Yet, still he squinted, somehow unsatisfied.

Kaito looked over the man before him from head to toe. After a moment, he murmured quietly.

"…Huh, is that what he was like?"

"Wh-where the hell am I? Even the afterlife ain't supposed to be this gloomy. And whaddaya think *you're* doin' here, Kaito? Hey. You little punk… You tryin' to get revenge or somethin'? Listen here, you—don't go tryin' any dumb shit!"

Suddenly, his father began carrying on and on. Even in death, his boiling point seemed to be as low as ever. And he'd always had a sense for when he was in danger, often to the point of paranoia.

Spit went flying as he spoke, but his eyes lacked the shade of madness they'd once possessed.

It was then that Kaito came to a realization. His father's madness had largely been the product of his rampant drug use. Even now, Kaito could see that the cruel, sadistic nature hidden within him was unchanged. His brawny figure and the readiness at which he hurt others were frightening, true. But that was the extent of it.

His father was screaming at him, but his expression was a far cry from the wicked one Elisabeth wore.

In fact, it didn't even compare to the gruesome images of the demons. It didn't compare to Clueless's dry, condescending gaze or to Marianne's tear-stained face. And it didn't even come close to Vlad's cheerful smile.

★   ★   ★

Kaito was dumbfounded.

"…You're not scary at all."

The instant he witnessed his father's clumsy, mundane fury, the fear in his heart vanished. His anger and bloodlust turned on their heads, as well, as he wondered if this was really the man he'd hated so passionately. And then, the tension that had been wound throughout his entire body just…dissolved. Losing the composure he'd held until then, he rubbed his eyes.

Sheesh, what's up with this? This guy? Is this really the guy?

"Hey, Kaito. What're you all quiet for? Gimme some answers, you little shit!"

Kaito couldn't even perceive the man standing before him as the same person who had killed him, the man he had feared, or the man who, by all rights, he should hate more than anyone else. Compared to this guy, the Earl had been a much more threatening foe.

Ohhh… I get it.

Thinking back on all the things he'd seen in this world, he found his answer.

I'm already numb.

He'd spent too much time around evils that surpassed human reason and too much time around the woman who fought them. The man who the old Kaito had been so terrified of no longer registered as someone to fear.

He finally realized something. The despotic, tyrannical "father" he'd despised so much no longer existed. The only one here was a small man, quick to anger and unable to control himself.

Watching his father continue to shout, Kaito spoke with quiet disappointment.

"...What, so that's all he was?"

In the next moment, Kaito broke out into laughter. His father looked confused. Kaito, finding this amusing, laughed even harder. As he clutched his sides with laughter, he could practically hear the invisible chains that had bound him shattering. This time, he truly, from the bottom of his heart, found it all to be so absurd.

Who would have guessed that the person who long held the key to Kaito's mental prison had been someone this trivial?

"I don't need him."

"Huh? What're you goin' on about? And why're you just ignorin' me and laughin' like a dumb-ass? You losin' it or somethin'?"

"I don't need someone like him. He's not worth the price."

His father was grabbing him by the collar, but Kaito just shrugged as he looked over his shoulder. Vlad frowned. The wound in his left wrist should have been deep, but it had already healed. *What a monster*, thought Kaito as he pointed a thumb at his father. With a clear heart, he made his declaration.

"Killing this guy isn't worth giving you my future."

Although he didn't understand the context, Kaito's father could tell that he was being mocked, and he raised a fist. But Vlad snapped his fingers, and Kaito's father's arm fell motionless. He looked at his arm in surprise. Vlad tilted his chin at Kaito, instructing him to continue. Kaito nodded and spoke.

"After I came to this world, I saw Hell…"

He'd seen people who crafted horrors, and he saw those who fought them. He'd seen sickening spectacles. He'd seen the weak get devoured. And amid all that, he'd somehow been able to survive. He'd had a teleportation circle carved in his own chest. He'd stopped running away. He'd helped defeat a demon. All that had been possible only thanks to the twisted ego of one woman.

The Torture Princess, Elisabeth Le Fanu. A woman as prideful as a wolf and as lowly as a sow.

The woman Kaito now served was more terrifying, more beautiful, and more steeped in sin than any other.

After all that, he couldn't remain shackled by a man as pathetic as his father.

He'd been killed. But so what.

He'd made a promise that was far more important than something as trivial as that.

"…But in that Hell, someone made a wish on my behalf. So no matter how impossible it is, I have to do everything I can to find happiness."

Kaito finished speaking his piece. Without a moment's hesitation, he called off his deal with Vlad.

Vlad crossed his arms in consideration. He gazed intently at Kaito's face and heaved a heavy sigh. Then, with theatrical exaggeration, he buried his face in his slender fingers and shook his head.

"It appears I approached you a hair too late."

"Yeah, a little. Well, maybe more than a little."

Kaito's response to Vlad's forlorn statement was lighthearted, and Vlad nodded in agreement.

Vlad then walked with a limp, as if he was grieving this outcome from the bottom of his heart. He drew near Kaito's father, then placed a hand on his shoulder. As he did, Kaito's father opened his mouth and began babbling loudly.

"Fuck's the matter with you you screwin' with me cut it out dammit fuckin' with me gonna kill you gonna fuckin' kill you—"

Apparently, Vlad had had restraints on his speech as well. No wonder he'd been so quiet. Knitting his brows in irritation, Vlad leaned toward Kaito's father's ear. As if approached by a carnivorous beast with fangs bared, Kaito's father immediately shut up. His earlobe had been warped in a fistfight, and Vlad's voice was sweet as he spoke into it.

"If you kill that thing in front of you once more, I will allow you to enjoy life anew. What do you say?"

After a moment of confusion, Kaito's father practically licked his lips. Quick on the uptake as ever. At the same time, Kaito turned on his heel and ran. An angry voice thick with avarice chased after him.

"Hold it, Kaito! Don't you fuckin' run from me!"

"I'm definitely gonna run, dumb-ass!"

As long as his brain wasn't atrophied, he could at least make sound decisions. And he had no intention of lying down and dying.

His father gave chase, shouting something incoherent. Kaito aimed for the entrance he had just come through. The maids did not stand in his way. He doubted he'd make it to Elisabeth alive, but if nothing else, even if he died, he had to stop Hina from shutting down. He should still be able to make it in time.

Then Vlad snapped his fingers. Azure petals and darkness swirled, and stakes pierced Kaito's feet.

"Gah-rgh!"

Kaito let out a scream of pain as he dropped to one knee. At the same time, his father caught up with him and hoisted him by the scruff of his neck. Trembling with rage, his father wrung his neck.

"Don't you look down on me, you no-good piece o' shit motherfucking brat! Don't you look down on me; don't you look down on meeeeeeeeeeeeeeee! Ahhhhhhhhh, you're a pain in my ass!"

Kaito tried to raise his hands and resist, but those were skewered as well. His arms drooped, covered in blood.

His field of view shrank and grew blurry. He recalled the unpleasant sensation of having his windpipe crushed. He was experiencing the same thing again. His body might be immortal, but at this rate, the bones in his neck would snap and his arteries would get punctured. If that happened, even he wouldn't survive.

Am I gonna get killed again?

He'd talked a good game, which made this all the more embarrassing. Just like last time, nobody came to save him. Even if he called out, there was nobody his voice could reach. There was nobody to come to his rescue.

This was the end for him, but he'd wanted to stop her, at least.

He recalled her gentle smile and her warm embrace. Why hadn't he run up to her and held her to keep her from leaving? A tear ran down his cheek as he whispered, his heart full of regret.

★   ★   ★

"...I'm sorry, Hina."

Suddenly, a stampeding sound came out of nowhere.

Kaito's father's grip loosened in surprise, and Kaito opened his eyes a sliver. His father was staring in the direction of the noise with his jaw hanging open. Curious, Kaito managed to look.

When he did, his jaw dropped, too.

Hina was barreling toward them, twirling her halberd like a tornado.

The maids rushed to stop her, but she blew them away with such vigor, it made one wonder what had become of her previous listless state. Her cheeks were flush and her eyes were glittering as she let out a strange voice.

"You called? You called for me? I just heard you calling for me, didn't I, Master Kaaaaiiiito?! I'm coming to save youuuuuuuuuuuuu!"

"Are you for real?"

Kaito muttered in astonishment. Sensing the danger he was in, his father pushed him aside and began running. Kaito fell hard toward the floor. But the impact never came. He found himself cradled in Hina's right arm. With her free left hand, she brandished her halberd.

"Huh?"

"For the sin of strangling Master Kaito, the punishment is death."

The top half of his father's body went flying and landed on its side. Blood and entrails splattered on the floor. In no time at all,

he was well past the point at which blood loss became fatal. He slumped over, motionless.

Without a shred of hesitation or doubt, and with a bit too much eagerness, the deed was done.

Still cradled in Hina's loving embrace, Kaito couldn't help but be astonished by what was happening. As if to avoid causing him any further shock, Hina plopped him on the ground, tossed aside her halberd, and held Kaito tight in her arms. She buried his face in her ample bosom and spoke with joy in her heart.

"Oh, Master Kaito! You saved me once more from the bleak abyss of death! How kind you are! I love you so! Your voice, along with its infinite mercy, has reached me! Oh, my beloved Master Kaito! As long as you wish it, I shall remain by your side for all eternity! I shall love you until my dying day, protecting you from all who would harm you!"

"Ha...ha-ha-ha..."

Kaito unwittingly broke into a weak laugh. It was all well and truly absurd. But little by little, joy welled up inside his chest. He'd thought that no one would come to save him. But that hadn't been true.

That wasn't true anymore.

He raised a bloody hand. Seeing it, Hina cried out in alarm. Ignoring her outburst, Kaito stroked her cheek. Not wanting to sully her perfect skin, he felt her warmth through his fingertips. After a little while, he breathed a sigh of relief.

"Master Kaito, what's wrong? Are you in pain?"

"I'm just glad you're alive. I'm so, so glad... And I'm sorry, Hina. I'm so sorry."

"M-Master Kaaiito! Please don't apologize! It's all right. Henceforth, and forever and for all of eternity, in sickness and in health, I will serve you with all my heart for as long as I live! Oh, this feeling of love! These emotions! Could they be the beginnings of maternal instinct?"

With an enraptured look on her face, Hina began muttering to herself. But then she turned, her expression fierce. A feral, murderous look flashed across her emerald-green eyes.

"...And it appears there's one brute left who would try to harm you."

Kaito looked up and saw Vlad, for whatever reason, trampling on his father's viscera with the soles of his leather shoes. As he looked at Vlad's icy profile, he felt his blood run cold. The man was livid. In his irritation, he looked like he planned on wasting no time in crushing Kaito and Hina.

"Fester and die, you son of a bitch."

"Hina, no!"

In the next moment, Hina vanished. Despite her injured state, she scooped up her halberd. Her pupils dilated as she drove it toward Vlad. Not even turning toward her, Vlad snapped his fingers.

Darkness and azure petals swirled, and a rotating saw appeared in the air.

The saw flew not at Hina but straight at Kaito. Vlad trained his apathetic eyes on Hina, testing her. She didn't hesitate even a moment. Casting her halberd aside, she wrenched her body into an impossible pose. She threw herself upon Kaito.

For a second, Kaito saw Neue's form superimposed on hers.

"Hina, no!"

At once, Kaito shoved Hina out of the saw's path.

"...What? Master...Kaito?"

Her eyes were wide, and her arms were outstretched. Kaito looked at her and smiled.

Then heat burned through his body. His stomach had been cleaved open. But although the rotating saw looked flashy, it turned out to be duller than Hina's halberd. Kaito had avoided being bisected, but his intestines still spilled from the wound. He collapsed without a word. Hina howled a crazed scream.

"Master...Kaito? Master Kaito, Master Kaito! *Noooooooooooo-oooo!*"

"...Urgh... Gah, hrk... Blech..."

Kaito could feel something warm pumping away from his heart. The gushing sound of his heartbeat was obnoxious. As he lay trembling on the floor, a thought faintly crossed his mind.

I hope...Hina will...take this...chance...to escape...... But I wouldn't...bet on it...

Based on her personality, he doubted she'd be able to leave him behind. He needed to find a way to tell her to run. But his voice no longer obeyed him. His field of view grew dark.

It should have been completely pitch-black, but light ran across his vision. What was that sensation? He remembered it from the time he'd activated a teleportation circle on his chest. It was the feeling of the magical energy in Elisabeth's blood, which was mixed with his own, writhing. On the brink of death, Kaito's soul was resonating with the powerful magic in the blood.

The memories in the blood began to resurface.

It was almost like his life was flashing before his eyes, like it did in stories.

But it was something else entirely, something sinister.

Endless corpses of the brutally slaughtered. Hundreds of crows taking flight. The frenzied masses, chanting in unison and crying out for blood. A girl, bound in a straitjacket, hanging in the air. A frail young child, peering out of her bedroom window.

A willowy man's fingers crept toward her bony shoulders draped in a negligee.

Her matted black hair shook as she gave a start. Flustered, she turned to look. Her gaze landed on the man, who raised his arms in surrender. Upon seeing his face, she breathed a sigh of relief.

"Oh, Uncle Vlad. Don't startle me like that."

"Ah, Elisabeth. My darling daughter. Have you been a good girl? You haven't been killing cats in secret again, have you?"

"I haven't. I don't do that anymore."

"I wonder about that. But don't worry. No matter what you do, I'll keep it a secret for you."

Her uncle's features much resembled hers, and his voice was full of joy over their reunion. For some reason, he always referred to Elisabeth as his daughter rather than his niece.

She was about to respond, but she then clamped her hand over her mouth. After a fit of dry coughing, she hacked up blood. Seeing her suffer, Vlad readied his proposition.

"O pitiful Elisabeth, born with incurable illness. Darling Elisabeth, she who possesses the same ruthless nature as I. You possess the *capability* yet are trapped on the brink of death. I have come to cure your ailment."

"Really? But Uncle, even the doctors say it can't be cured. And what do you mean by 'capability'?"

"You will eventually understand in time. Now come, take this. But just like I keep quiet about your mischief, you mustn't tell anyone about this."

Her uncle put his index finger to his lips and winked. Elisabeth nodded. Vlad then praised her with a pat on the head and retrieved something from his bag.

"With this, you shall surely lead a more enjoyable life than any other."

In her outstretched hands, he deposited a gray lump of meat. It was shaped like a human heart.

After eating the meat, Elisabeth made it safely to her sixteenth year.

Everyone rejoiced at her miraculous survival. But then, as if in payment for that miracle, both of her parents passed away. One night, their carriage drove off a cliff. The cause of the fall was undetermined, but right before the accident, an elderly individual reported seeing a massive black dog by the side of the road.

On the night of their funeral, Elisabeth sat by her window as she'd done in her youth, clad in her mourning dress. A pale finger crept toward her shoulder. With a start, she lifted her tear-stained face.

Before her stood her uncle, dressed in black. He should have been away, traveling the countryside.

"Uncle Vlad."

"Ah, Elisabeth! I'm so glad to see you alive and well, my darling!"

Not noticing how unnatural his greeting was, Elisabeth rushed to hug her beloved uncle. But all of a sudden, he began clapping. She stopped in her tracks, her eyes wide. Even though her parents had just died, he was clapping as if to say that there was nothing to be done about it.

"...Uncle?"

"The demon's flesh was able to take root within you!"

Elisabeth couldn't understand what he was talking about. But upon seeing him again in the moonlight, she noticed something. His face was far too young and much too handsome for his age.

And it was wicked, besides. He continued, his voice like that of a child inviting another to mischief.

"Elisabeth, by now, no human illness can kill you. But from this moment on, you'll have to hurt others and offer up their pain, and the discord in their souls, to your body. If you don't, the demon flesh within you will rot, and you will die, racked with gut-wrenching agony. No, no, there's no need to be afraid. Be at ease, my pitiful, lovely Elisabeth."

Vlad grinned as he basked in the moonlight. He continued speaking, a wicked grin on his face.

"Your parents left you the population of the fiefdom, throngs of subjects to indulge yourself in. Until you have licked your plate clean, until you have feasted to your heart's content, you should eat as much as you can."

Elisabeth sensed that her uncle's words were no jest. Belatedly, she also realized something. That thing she had eaten all those years ago had been something forbidden, something that should have never been consumed.

Trembling, Elisabeth clutched her shoulders. Her uncle smiled as he spoke again.

★　　★　　★

"Yes, Elisabeth Le Fanu. Now you can become a greedier sow than any other."

A few days later, Elisabeth became unable to bear the pain that racked her body. With her uncle Vlad's help, she used a real torture device for the very first time and committed her first murder.

She ripped out the guts of a living person with a windlass and slaughtered a young girl in a hanging cage, weeping and vomiting all the while. As she piled up bodies by the day, Vlad laughed loudly by her side.

"Very good, Elisabeth, very, very good! More, Elisabeth, more! What do you think, beloved daughter of mine? Aren't you having fun?"

"…Yes, maybe… You might be right…"

With tears in her eyes, she looked at the corpses of those she'd killed, those who had hated her, resented her, and wanted her to die. The more she wept and apologized, the more their hatred grew, expanding without limit.

Before long, the poisonous flower was in full bloom.

She'd tried to kill herself over a dozen times, but Vlad kept her in check. It was only after meeting the demonic friends he'd assembled that she finally stopped resisting.

"Weep or rejoice as I may, the results remain unchanged."

She accepted her lot in life. She draped herself in a dress she weaved with magic, used the energies she'd accumulated to summon torture devices, and slaughtered the inhabitants of her castle town.

★   ★   ★

As she violated her innocent subjects, she sat alone in the throne room and swirled a glass of wine back and forth.

"What kind of person apologizes when eating pork or feasting on steak? No amount of tears that I shed, no amount of regret that I feel will change who I am or what I've done. As such, I have made my choice. I choose to be proud.

"I choose to rejoice as I make all the people of this world into my sacrifices.

"Why should I weep when I make victims of others? Why should I apologize?! I shall laugh as I slaughter you. I shall line you up on my plate. I shall take pleasure in devouring you. And I shall rub my belly when I've eaten my fill. However, you all have the right to kill me. I shall show you no mercy as I consume you, but the day will come when the devourer and the devoured trade places, and I shall die at the stake."

"Rebuke me. Hate me. Curse my name and condemn me to Hell!"

"I am the Torture Princess, Elisabeth Le Fanu!"

"I am the proud wolf and the lowly sow, forsaken by all of creation!"

After that, Elisabeth gave rise to myriad blood-soaked legends, accumulating magical power comparable to that of the strongest demon. Once more, she became a worthy successor to Vlad. But for some reason, she suddenly revolted against her self-proclaimed foster father.

She laughed as she skewered his underlings with thousands upon thousands of stakes.

"Why, hello, Vlad. Don't tell me you truly believed the day you met your match would never come, did you? 'Tis your judgment day. Your fate and mine are the same—to be killed like the swine we are."

The two of them struck at once, each downing the other, and they were both captured by the Church.

Perhaps her heinous deeds, committed without fear of God, were all for the sake of extending her own life.

Or perhaps they were for the sake of defeating her "father," whose power and allies had grown well past the point where any normal person could stand against him.

Her motives would remain a mystery.

"...Gah, hah!"

Kaito coughed up blood as he came to his senses. It appeared he'd been fortunate and vomited up the blood that had pooled in the back of his throat. The sudden pain had shaken his soul out of its shocked state. Elisabeth's memories faded, leaving him unable to see them anymore. Reality, along with the fact that he was steadily losing blood, came rushing back to him.

The floor felt warm, like a blanket, and strangely soft. His senses seemed to be failing him. The blood he was lying in felt strangely comfortable.

Closing his eyes again, Kaito thought back on the memories he'd just witnessed.

...That was rough; I'll give you that. Given your circumstances, no one could've saved you.

Resisting the urge to surrender himself to sleep, Kaito opened his eyes. His vision was blurry, and he couldn't make much out in the darkness. But he could tell that Hina was waving her halberd and fighting something off.

She was protecting him. His head swimming, Kaito tried to think.

Even God turned away from you. And yet, you intentionally... You chose to become the Torture Princess. Man, I can't even begin to understand that.

Kaito reached out his hand. It sank into the sticky pool of blood surrounding him. He stretched out his arm again, searching for a dry section of floor. His arm trembled as he frantically began moving it.

Even for the sake of living or fighting back...I still don't get how you could choose something like that so easily... So brazenly...

As he squirmed about on the floor, Kaito moved his fingertips once more. Ignoring his pain and the blood he was losing, he wriggled on the floor like a worm. Perhaps thinking he was trying to flee, Vlad laughed and muttered.

"It seems your master intends to abandon you, even as you fight for him. Do you wish to continue in spite of this?"

"Master Kaito is fleeing? How wonderful! Then I shall buy him as much time as he needs!"

The metallic *clang* of blade against blade rang out. All the while, Kaito continued crawling around. He dragged streaks of blood across the ground, and as he connected line to line, he let out a small laugh.

"But man... I guess we did have one thing in common after all. Like...birds of a feather, they say."

It was just as Clueless had said. There was one area in which Kaito and Elisabeth resembled each other quite a bit. Kaito extended his arm a little more. Straining his exposed innards as he worked, he wrote a glyph.

"I'm already dead...and back when I was alive, I never did manage to get in a solid hit. But you're still alive, so...while you still can...go give your 'dad' one good punch."

Kaito connected the beginning and end of the circle with his finger. His work finally done, he collapsed. He could feel the blood burn with magical energy. Vlad, finally realizing what was going on, shouted.

"...That's—"

In front of Kaito, *Elisabeth's summoning circle had been completed.*

Over the course of his first life, he'd developed a certain skill—he never forgot any information he'd learned through pain. He'd taken advantage of that by carving a map of the castle's underground tunnels in his skin so he wouldn't get lost.

And he'd once gotten *Elisabeth to carve a teleportation circle on his chest.*

He'd drawn the teleportation circle just as he remembered it, and it began undulating wildly. The blood flowed, full of Elisabeth's magical energy. It glimmered, its vivid crimson hue resembling melted rubies.

Aided by the light of the circle, Kaito could finally make out what was going on in the room. Vlad was firing off attacks, his face full of impatience, but Hina was somehow holding him at bay. Kaito coughed up blood as he let out a scream.

"And then, once you've cleaned up this mess, you can go straight to Hell like you swore! *ELISABEEEEEEEEEEEEEEE EEEEEEEEEEETH!*"

As Kaito screamed, darkness exploded from the circle. Crimson flower petals spiraled around the room like a blood-soaked hurricane.

A long dress fluttered amid the tempest of darkness and petals. Its scarlet interior swirled across his view. A fair woman appeared, puffing out her buxom leather-bound bust. Her sleek black hair wafted behind her, and her crimson gaze settled on Kaito.

She landed atop Kaito's blood and guts sporting her bondage-style dress and devilishly good looks.
It made for a beautiful, warped image.

In her hand, she held the Executioner's Sword of Frankenthal.

"Hello there, Vlad."

Elisabeth, immediately grasping the situation, laughed a dark laugh. Her lips twisted in the most wicked yet sublime way imaginable. Vlad recoiled a step.
Elisabeth, drenched in blood, was currently free of the

Church's shackles. Not only was Vlad shackled, but the Kaiser wasn't by his side. She licked her lips as she eyed her prey.

She raised the Executioner's Sword of Frankenthal aloft. Crimson flower petals and darkness spiraled around the blade. She then brought the shining sword down, as if conducting an execution.

"Now die alone—forsaken by heaven and earth and all of creation!"

Chains appeared from every direction and quickly filled the room. Hina was lying on the ground, and they flew over her head, shredded the maids, and twined around Vlad like a serpent. He struggled and fought, trying to break the chains with his own darkness and azure petals. But the chains wound around him faster than he could cut. His bones creaked as they bore down on his skin.

"Tch... Ah, rrrgh..."

He hung in the air, suspended by chains as Elisabeth had once been. Crimson petals piled up around him, like a massive bouquet for the dead. Then, in an instant, they melted and transformed into a platform with a stake. The chains bound Vlad to it. Elisabeth swung her sword again, and crimson flames burned in its wake. It was not a demonic flame but a mortal one.

He burned in the flames of man, as if he was being judged by the people.

"To think I would be done in...by something like this... This is a cruel joke, Elisabeth..."

Heavy darkness and azure petals whirled around Vlad. But

the chains remained unbroken, and the fire spread to the tail of his elegant coat. His flesh began to burn. He opened his eyes in disbelief.

His sapphire stare was trained on Elisabeth. She returned it with a smile that seemed almost kind. Vlad frantically looked about, as if he'd only just grasped his situation.

Suddenly, he'd found himself trapped within the jaws of death for the very first time.

A bleak murmur dribbled from his mouth, as if imploring her.

"Elisabeth... Elisabeth... Elisabeth... Elisabeth..."

"Despots are killed, tyrants are hung, and slaughterers are slaughtered. Such are the ways of the world. The demise of torturers should be garnished with their own screams as they sink to Hell with no chance for salvation. Only at such a time is a torturer's life truly complete—so meet your fate, you vile man. I have no intention of fleeing. I shall follow you shortly."

The tips of Vlad's long hair caught ablaze. No longer keeping up appearances, his body convulsed. The platform creaked a little. Then his skin burst into flames. He burned like an ordinary man, and Elisabeth made her declaration.

"*Death by Burning*—a fitting end for you and me."

"*ELISABEEEEEEEEEEEEEEEEEEEEEEEEEEEEEEEEEE EEEEEEEEEEEEEEEEEEEEEEEEEEEEEEEEEEEEEEEETH!*"

As Vlad let out a resentful scream, the blaze swallowed him.

The flames caused his face to bulge and sizzle. His skin turned to carbon. And eventually, his entire body burned away. All that remained were bones, and the chains mercilessly shattered them. He became white ash, then scattered into the air and vanished on

the wind. Vlad Le Fanu had become nothing more than another victim claimed by the Torture Princess, Elisabeth Le Fanu.

And that was how the man who had served as the Kaiser and created the Torture Princess met his end.

All that remained was Elisabeth, standing alone, ever the picture of regality.

Amid the heat from the flames still lingering in the room, she closed her eyes and looked up at the sky. Her black hair drifted behind her, and a crimson flower petal fell from her skin.

Having defeated her lifelong foe, Elisabeth took a short breath, exhaled, and opened her eyes.

"How weak!"

She thrust her fist skyward as she shouted in pure satisfaction.

Out of all the things she could have chosen to say, that's *what she went with?*

As he lamented her choice of words, Kaito's consciousness slipped away.

Kaito Sena

A young man, brutally killed after a life of abuse. He is summoned by Elisabeth and made to work as her servant. Due to his experiences in life, strong emotions such as fear, anger, and hatred make him unusually calm.

Epilogue

"Deeeeeeeeeeeeeeeeeeeeeeeeeeeeeeeeeeeeeeeeeeeeeelicious!"

Elisabeth gripped her fork and knife as she shouted with glee.

Laid out before her were jellied beef tongue, gizzard rillettes, kidney pie with a blue-cheese sauce, and tripe cutlets.

"I am grateful for your praise, Lady Elisabeth."

"Man, your reactions are always way over-the-top when it comes to food."

Hina smiled and gave a tidy bow. Kaito stood next to her, holding a wine bottle with both hands. Each time Elisabeth emptied her glass, he mechanically moved to refill it.

His task hardly took his humanity into account. His poured the wine with dead eyes, not giving a damn about the wine's flavor. Apparently, though, as long as the food was good, Elisabeth didn't much care about the quality of the liquor. She happily drained her glass. *At least my job is easy*, he thought. He looked down at his clothes and sighed.

He would have really appreciated it if she got him something nicer to wear than his butler uniform.

Ignoring his complaints, Elisabeth devoured the spread. But as she finished her final plate and Kaito moved to refill her glass, she suddenly spoke.

"Have you no misgivings?"

"About what?"

He immediately returned her question. Still holding the wine bottle, he waited for her reply.

✦   ✦   ✦

A few days had passed since they'd purged the Kaiser and returned to the stone castle.

This was the first time Elisabeth had spoken on the matter.

That night, after being carried back to the castle, Kaito had confessed that he'd temporarily accepted Vlad's invitation. But Elisabeth had simply treated his wounds, then tossed him into bed. He'd immediately slipped into a comatose state, and Hina had held his hand through the night while Elisabeth delivered her report to the Church.

The following day, his usual warped yet not-unpleasant lifestyle awaited him. He'd decided not to mention prior events, so when Elisabeth broached the subject on her own, he was taken by surprise. There were too many possible answers to her question about his "misgivings," so he simply tilted his head.

Elisabeth raised a slender finger.

"First, the matter of the Church's custody."

"Oh, well, misgivings or not, people from other worlds are still rare, right? And that place seems full of holes, so if there was anyone else like Clueless there, I'd be done for. It's not like I'd have any way to resist, so because I can't guarantee that I'm not gonna become a lab rat, I have no plans of fleeing to the Church at the moment."

"At the moment, eh?"

"Well, yeah. If I really felt like you were gonna die and I was gonna follow shortly after, then who knows. I might well go sobbing to the Church and beg them for help."

"Ah, how very like you."

"Yeah, I'd rather not accompany you to Hell."

"And I would rather not have you."

Elisabeth responded in a muted tone, then shook her empty glass. Obeying her unvoiced order, Kaito filled it to the brim. Spinning the glass as she spoke, Elisabeth asked her next question.

"Second, then. Are you truly okay with *that*?"

"Oh...yeah. *That*. Yeah, I'm fine with that as it is."

"I see. Well, if you say so, then that is that."

Unlike Kaito, who had survived due to Elisabeth giving him a blood transfusion, his father's doll body had lost all its blood, and his soul had disappeared. Elisabeth could have summoned it again, but Kaito had turned her down. On his request, though, she'd recovered the doll's body, and Kaito had buried it behind the castle.

The burial had had no meaning. Yet, for some reason, Kaito had wanted to do it anyway.

And so he did.

Kaito had no plans to visit his father's grave. In time, it would grow over with weeds or flowers as they sprouted naturally. That was for the best.

That thought alone had allowed him to sort out his feelings.

Here in front of him sat Elisabeth again. It was her egotism that had set all of this in motion. It was the Torture Princess who had thrust herself into this insane situation and she who had forced this second life upon him.

Kaito shrugged, then spoke to her casually.

"And hey, you bringing me back to life and summoning me here must have been some kind of fate... So until you start walking the road to Hell, I'll try and stick by your side for as long as I can, even if I'm the only one."

Elisabeth would die alone. Not even a demon would be by her side then.

But perhaps it wouldn't be so bad for one human to stay by her side until that fateful day arrived.

Throughout Elisabeth Le Fanu's bloody life, she was accompanied by a single foolish servant.

Kaito thought that sounded just fine.

Elisabeth cast a sidelong glance at him. She then shrugged and gave a catlike laugh.

"And what of it? Am I supposed to be overjoyed at the prospect of being served till death by an unfaithful servant like you? One who can't even cook?"

"Man, you ask a lot for someone who can only summon people from other worlds who can't cook organs worth a damn."

"I'll kill you for that. Painfully. But...very well. Bring me that thing, that one talent you possess."

"Aye aye, cap'n. It's been a while."

He obeyed her command and returned the wine bottle to its bowl. He then picked up the earthenware pot from the tub of ice it was chilling in. Hina, unable to restrain herself, bubbled with excitement as she peered at it.

Watching the other two crane their necks, Kaito whipped off the lid.

"Ah, so that's what Master Kaito's special *purin* is like! How splendid!"

"Indeed, it jiggles so wonderfully. I crave it from time to time. Now, without further ado…"

Kaito gazed at them, Elisabeth readying her spoon and Hina unable to contain her excitement. It was then that he realized something. He felt around his face with caution.

Sure enough, a natural smile had spread across it.

…*Oh, so that's what that feels like.*

He thought back to the promise he'd made Neue. Then he calmly surveyed the scene before him.

Elisabeth was there, and so was Hina. He hoped these chaotic, happy days would continue. For the first time in his life, he prayed that he wouldn't lose them, even as the battles heated up. And to that end, he planned to do everything in his power.

To fulfill his promise to Neue and to keep the promise he'd just made to Elisabeth.

The Torture Princess, Elisabeth Le Fanu, had summoned him from another world.

She would one day die alone, forsaken by all of creation, and descend to Hell.

But they still had some time before then.

Afterword

Good day, and to those of you I haven't met before, it's a pleasure to meet you. I'm Keishi Ayasato.

Thank you all very much for purchasing *Torture Princess*. Some of you will say, "But I'm just skimming it at the bookstore!" To those people, this is the part where I cling to your leg and beg you not to leave it behind. My grandpa said that something good will happen if you take it to the register with you. More specifically, you could get a +3 bonus to Luck. As far as the accuracy of that statement goes, I have no comment.

Torture Princess is the first book I had the honor of writing for MF Bunko J. Because it was the first, I was pretty nervous. I sincerely hope you liked it, even if only a little.

The idea of the Torture Princess, a wicked, beautiful woman of noble birth who commands countless torture devices, was one that I'd wanted to write about for a while. However, I'd never been able to come up with a reason for the protagonist to be with her or why he would continue serving her, so the story never really took form. It was when my editor suggested I write a story combining dark elements with the *isekai* genre that a light went on in my mind. *Ah*, I thought, *the premise can be that she summons him after he dies and forces him to work for her!* After that, I was able to write Kaito and Elisabeth's story without a hitch.

★　　★　　★

If you don't mind, I would be thrilled to tell you what happens next in the tale of the sinner who awaits death by burning at her own hands and the boy who gets a second chance at life. Incidentally, I wrote a limited-edition booklet that you can find at animate, describing a day in the life of the aforementioned two, as well as Hina, the doting maid who showers the protagonist with all the love of a blushing bride. As a bonus, the Butcher shows up, too. Skipping it won't affect your enjoyment of the sequel, but if you're interested, please check it out (I'm the type to toss in advertisements at key moments like this). Please take a look, even if all you do is admire the beautiful cover Saki Ukai drew for it. But most of all, I hope from the bottom of my heart that if I successfully manage a sequel, it will catch your eye. Oh, that would make me so happy.

Please, I beg of you.

I'm almost out of room in the afterword, so I guess this is the part where I start thanking people.

Saki Ukai, thank you so much for your beautiful character designs and illustrations. When I first saw Elisabeth's design, it took my breath away. To my designer and my publisher, your suggestions were invaluable, and to my editor O, I wish to extend my deepest gratitude.

And finally, to my readers, my sincerest thanks. There is no greater pleasure for an author than to have people read their work. I will put everything I have into making my next story entertaining, so it would bring me great joy if you all looked forward to it.

And with that, I hope we will meet again.